The Spirit
and the Skull

Books by J. M. Hayes

The Mad Dog & Englishman Mysteries
Mad Dog & Englishman
Prairie Gothic
Plains Crazy
Broken Heartland
Server Down
English Lessons

Other Novels
The Grey Pilgrim
The Spirit and the Skull

The Spirit and the Skull

J. M. Hayes

Poisoned Pen Press

Library of Congress Catalog Card Number: 2014931731

ISBN: 9781464202827   Hardcover
       9781464202858   Trade Paperback

Poisoned Pen Press
6962 E. First Ave., Ste. 103
Scottsdale, AZ 85251
www.poisonedpenpress.com
info@poisonedpenpress.com

Printed in the United States of America

For Karl, who introduced me to the tundra and The People.
For Egon, Hal, and Jon, who shared the magic.
And in memory of Claire for making it possible.

Whoso neglects learning in his youth
Loses the past and is dead for the future.
—Euripides

Unthinkable

My shadow ran ahead of me, winking in and out. Low clouds scraped the top of the rocky slope I struggled to climb, allowing occasional flashes of sunlight. I hurried, bearing important news for my band. Nightmares I already couldn't remember had forced me from my sleeping robes that morning and sent me racing through the dwarf willows along the banks of a stream filled with glacier melt. I felt desperate to share what I'd discovered on my scout. Why hadn't I found the band already? They should have come farther than this. What slowed them? If we weren't well south of this tundra before another vicious winter hit, we'd freeze and starve again.

The slope grew steeper as I scrambled over weathered shale and clawed my way up unstable conglomerate. The peak stood at least twenty times my height. Not something I wanted to climb, especially as the rock on this weathered ridge crumbled beneath me as I put my weight on it. The moss- and lichen-covered surface tumbled me back down toward the stream, even though I grabbed at it with fresh enthusiasm as the lion followed me out of the willows. He snarled and I attacked the rock face with renewed vigor, grasping any stone that might lift me higher than he could climb.

The lion was old, but still deadly enough to steal my life with one snap of his jaws. A young lion would have brought me down already, though a healthier lion probably wouldn't have bothered with prey as ancient and scrawny as I. This fellow sported as many gray hairs as gold, tottering after me on aching joints. The wind tore at me, trying to gift me to the starving beast. A sudden burst of chilling rain stole more feeling from my frozen fingers and made the rocks even slicker before racing away to the south.

Fighting the beast was out of the question while I had the option of escaping. So I'd shoved my spear in the rolled-up sleeping robe tied to my pack and slung over my shoulders to free my hands for the climb. Now the foot of its shaft dragged on the rocks and threatened my balance. As I tried to adjust it, my bow began slipping. I grabbed for it. Releasing the cliff put too much weight on my caribou-hide boots. The niche that had held them crumbled. Suddenly, I dangled by one hand over empty air, close to falling and rewarding the old lion in spite of his clumsy stalk.

"No!" I shouted at the lion and the howling wind. "You can't have me. I'm Raven, Hawk Talon's son—Spirit Man to Stone's band, translator of The Mother's will, messenger for the spirits, and scout for my people. I've discovered the pass between the glaciers. Grandfather Eagle swore that it leads to The Mother's promised land. She won't let you take me now."

The cat jumped for me, raking his claws across the stones far below where I hung. The cobbles failed under him, too, but he licked his lips, showing worn teeth, still sharp enough to tear me apart.

I surprised myself by laughing. What a ridiculous situation. Even if The Mother answered my prayer and directed the lion away, it wouldn't matter. The fall would kill me. Why were the spirits allowing this when I'd learned so much my band needed to hear?

The wind slacked and I twisted back to the rock face, saw a solid-looking stone, and grabbed it with my bow-encumbered hand. My feet swung back to the crevasse that had failed me moments before. It was deeper now. It took my feet and accepted its share of my weight. My perch felt safe again…for the moment.

Exhausted, shaking from my brush with death, too many years, and too little sleep, I hugged the rock, drawing strength from Grandmother Earth. Gradually, my breathing and pulse returned to normal. I looked up. I was almost at the top. Places for hands and feet were everywhere. I would test them carefully, calm myself, and climb this last bit more intelligently than I had the first. My right foot explored the surface and found a stone it couldn't stomp free. My left foot lifted to another. My hands felt above. Here. Here. Over there. In moments, my shadow and I lay safe atop the peak.

The sun must have grown curious to see how I was doing. I shook my fist at him. "All right, no thanks to you."

When I looked down, the lion had vanished. I thought he might be searching the ridge for an easier way up. But there was nothing between me and its slopes to hide him. He must have crept back into the tangle of dwarf willows. They were dense enough to mask him, but from this angle, I might be able to see a beast that size moving through them.

And then, there he was, bolting from the willows on the other side of the stream. Moving faster and with more determination than when he'd chased me. Another gust of wind rolled across the willows and I saw why. A great bear stood near the stream's bank, head raised, his eyes looking straight at me. The willows closed back over him and I watched the lion flee toward distant green hills, the pain in his joints forgotten in his eagerness to avoid the great bear.

Maybe I shouldn't be so upset with the spirits. If I hadn't needed to avoid the elderly cat I might have run straight into the bear. I'd been scraped, scratched, and badly frightened, but I was alive.

I checked the willows again, hoping to see which direction the bear was going. Upstream, I'd thought. But if I was wrong, I'd have a far better chance of living long enough to deliver my messages by staying on this ridge.

I spun in a slow circle searching for some sign of my band and found nothing, not unless some of those distant clouds were smoke from our fires. I couldn't tell, but the band had to be somewhere in that direction. I scrambled over a few prominent boulders, found the gravel surface that topped these ridges, and began running again.

Grandfather Eagle's visit to our camp is among my first childhood memories. The famed old Spirit Man traveled among The People during my fifth summer, persuading us to make this journey. The Mother had appeared to him in visions and shown him a new land where rolling prairies lay, filled to overflowing with the herds that grazed them. There, we'd find mountains rich in game and beauty, lakes and great rivers bountiful with fish and fowl. Grandfather Eagle told us that land had gentle winters and warm summers. Rains watered abundant grass, fruit and nut trees, and bushes hung thick with sweet berries in their season. The Mother, he explained, had told him The People should go and claim it. We would grow fat, raise many children, and dominate our enemies. The land she showed Grandfather Eagle was nearly empty—waiting for our arrival. The journey would be difficult and take many years. We must travel north and east across country that was cold and unforgiving before finally turning south and eventually reaching the place of her bountiful gift. Grandfather Eagle explained that we had no choice. The Mother would no longer smile on us if we failed to accept. She'd abandon us then and give her promised land to another tribe.

Well, I'd lived more than forty summers and we were still on our way. But now, within reach. I'd found the pass between the mountains of ice. Finally, we could go south, leave this cold, cruel, but hauntingly beautiful land.

The cloud's mists chilled me as my running shadow came and went. The rocks bruised my feet, even encased in my tough skin boots, freshly stuffed and padded with soft grasses that morning. Rolling, deceptively beautiful meadows surrounded my path on every side. They seemed an inviting place to run. Up close, I knew they were harsh and uncaring places.

The meadows below, stretching from horizon to horizon, were sedges. Great clumps, tussocks that grew like the spray that forms when a heavy stone is thrown in water. Only the center of each clump could be walked on. The earth beneath never fully melted. In between lay mud. Or deep holes where frozen ice wedges melted—hidden traps to catch the careless. They might only swallow a man's foot and fill his boot with chilling muck, or they could use his momentum, grab a leg, and snap bone.

From the path along the ridge, I could see the ice wedges, regular multi-sided lines around segments of grass. But from the height of a man's eyes, the wedges and their holes, as well as the weak edges of clumps that might merely trip you, became nearly invisible. At least until you started crossing the tundra and the meadow revealed its true nature. If that wasn't sufficient, the tundra housed enough mosquitoes to bleed a man dry, or drive him mad, in moments.

Our band tried to avoid traveling across these tundra prairies. We preferred the twisting courses of streams and adventures encountered among the willows. At least their groves supplied edible plants and small game as well as hiding the beasts that hunted man. Where the willows grew, no more than half again a man's height, the soil drained and we could walk rather than stumble. They couldn't hide mammoths or mastodons. Nor great bears, if they stood on their hind legs. But great bears traveled on all fours.

A great bear is surprisingly nimble and can move with hardly any sound. Not enough to be heard by a man absorbed in the conversation between wind and willows, or of water and stones. I might step around a clump of bright green leaves and find a bear, even a small bear, and die quickly. Safety among the willows could only be achieved by traveling in a well-armed group. Then, we might stop a bear. Or better still, persuade it to search for easier prey.

We traveled these ridges when they went where we wanted. The rocky soil drained well—no mud and rare ice. Best of all, the wind swept away most of the mosquitoes, making ridges near streams ideal camping spots. This ridge curved a little, but offered a surprisingly even path in the direction I wanted to go.

I followed it, settling into an easy pace that ate the distance I'd traveled on my scout.

I carried good news, important news. First, the pass between the glaciers. Then I'd found a family. They'd paused in The People's great migration, waiting to see whether their child, who'd slipped and fallen into a deep pool, would live or die. Die, I feared. Still, I'd bent to sprinkle him with pollen and blow good air into his tiny lungs. He hadn't responded. He still breathed, but when I peeled his eyelids back, no one remained behind them. I thought his spirit had already left his little body. I didn't tell his family. I gave them my sympathy and left them with good wishes. They already knew better. They just weren't ready to admit it to themselves.

They'd fed me, both food and information. Their own band had gone ahead two days before. Their scout had also found the place where the herds moved south through the mountains and the ice. A passage, they thought, and so did I. Summer still ruled the tundra. The sun burned all day, though sometimes behind clouds of icy rain and snow. Before long, the sun would desert this land, giving way to winter. Then the sun would leave for what seemed like forever. Our band had lost four elders and six children to last winter's long cold night. And a woman in childbirth. We suffered, with never enough to eat or enough fuel to keep us warm.

Two elders, Sings While He Works and Hungry Woman, chose to "go hunting" in the snowy dark because they were no longer productive enough and because we didn't have sufficient food. Both those elders were younger than I.

A boy and a girl went with them, One Arm and Walks in Darkness. Those children left because one had a withered limb and the other could hardly see. They also drained us, failing to earn their keep. Though what child ever did? Or what adult, on every day in every season? Our band leader, Stone, spent long hours staring at me, considering my worth and age as he made his choices—deciding who to not-so-gently persuade that the time had come to die for the good of the rest. Another hard winter on this tundra and he might decide I should go scouting in the frozen night, even if my skills hadn't begun to desert me. I was old, so it might not matter whether I was the band's best scout and still a skilled hunter. I could no longer outrun the young men, but I could run farther. I knew herbs and potions. Best, I read the signs the spirits sent us. I cajoled them, or appeased them, or caused them to look on our band and do us good instead of harm. But Stone had begun to doubt me last winter, when the storms wouldn't stop and our food was nearly gone. That was when Stone walked among the band considering who should live and who could be done without.

It has always been the custom of The People to cull themselves when necessary. Stone and his followers argued that they, the ones who produced the most, needed more food than the rest of us. There was truth in that, but I always felt we should have shared more equally and then all of us could have survived the winter. Those elders and crippled children hadn't reached a point where they contributed nothing. I spoke up about it. I told stories of heroic sacrifice and remarkable deeds from unexpected sources. It didn't stop the four from going into the snow, and it made Stone complain openly about what I provided for the band.

After finding the family, I came across a lone mammoth. She grazed among the willows, a huge old cow, injured and unable to put weight on one of her rear legs. I looked her over closely. She raised her trunk and bellowed, demanding I stay away. Angry in her pain, she threatened me. But her leg and age prevented her from charging. Gray and scared, she could only shamble. If we took her before some other band found her, before she fell and couldn't get up and wolves or a great bear claimed her, we could harvest all the meat we could carry. Enough for us to push ahead. To push south, without needing to pause so often to hunt to feed ourselves. She might speed our arrival in the land of which Grandfather Eagle spoke.

That mammoth, though her meat would be tough, would also provide her hide to make us another great tent. We needed it. We were crowded. We'd lost tents to the savage winds of winter. Many of the remaining were thin and tattered. The cow's ivory would make fine spear points and arrowheads. Perhaps I could carve a piece in The Earth Mother's image to honor how she shared her abundance. If so, she might finally notice me again, hear my prayers. She might even smile on me and send me women, as she had before I lost my first carving of her, and the woman who wore it.

By the time I reached the end of the ridge I knew where our band had camped. The sky had blown itself clear of clouds, and smoke blew from a ridge on the other side of the river.

I scrambled down, weaving through the willows to the stream's bank, stripped off my skins, bundled them with my bedding and weapons, then waded into the icy water.

I shook uncontrollably by the time I emerged from the stream. My manhood had shriveled to nothing and my sack was empty, its contents having gone to hide in the warmth of my body. I was glad Blue Flower and the other women couldn't see me like this—skinny, old, covered with as many scars as the mammoth cow, and, worse, sexless. Even though I remember more than forty summers, I still wanted young women to smile at me. But I didn't want them to laugh.

I'm unusual. Most of our band seldom bathed on the tundra. I hated the cold, but I loved the feeling of being clean. Normally, I would have found a warm place on a rock or in the soft grass at the side of the stream where I could stretch out and let the sun dry and warm me, if the mosquitoes cooperated. But not today.

I stacked my possessions on a boulder and briefly considered daubing myself with mud and letting it dry to keep the mosquitoes away. The day was growing warmer and there'd be more of them, especially down here. But I couldn't afford to sweat and let dried soil revert to grit and gravel that rubbed me raw. Still damp, I struggled into my skins and leather boots, packing them with soft fresh grass for padding. Wet grass, though, cold and not so comfortable. I settled my pack over one shoulder and my bow and quiver on the other.

For a moment, the wind paused. Instead of its moan, I heard another…coming from the ridge that smoked. Human voices. Not moaning, wailing. Crying out in mourning for the dead.

I threw myself through the willows to the place where the sedges began. By then, the wind returned, masking what I'd heard. I used my spear like a walking stick, testing the tussocks and the holes between them. I was in luck. The smoking ridge rose from the false meadow only a dozen bow shots away. I probably shouldn't have run across it, but what I'd heard added yet another reason to reach my band as soon as possible. I threw myself across the sedges, picking my path.

The mosquitoes found me. Eyes narrowed, mouth closed to keep from inhaling a cloud of them, I danced across the tundra. By the time I reached the bottom of the ridge, I was a mass of welts.

◇◇◇

The band mourned for Tall Pine, one of our leaders. The girl, Down, told me after seeing me cross the spine of the ridge above our camp. Her sharp eyes caught my silhouette against the sky and recognized my gait. She left the wailing women and raging men and met me on the first shelf above camp. It should have been Stone or Bull Hump or Takes Risks—our other leaders. Or at least another competent warrior. Instead, Down's was the observant eye that picked me out and knew I was no threat.

"It's Tall Pine," she told me.

"Dead?" I frowned. "You know better than to name the dead."

"Tall Pine," she said again.

I shook my head but didn't repeat my warning. She'd heard me use the names of the dead often enough and was no more frightened of their spirits than I. In fact, I'd never known Down to show less bravery than the most courageous member of our band.

"Murdered," she added.

I took a deep breath. According to the spirit's rules, murder made it even more important not to name him. But how could it be murder? The People didn't kill each other. Not that way.

Men sometimes fought for power or women, though rarely to the death. According to The People's laws, a formal challenge had to be issued first. And accepted. Then, if someone died, that person had given permission for their life to be taken.

Bands occasionally quarreled and fought and, sometimes, people died as a result. But, again, only after the issuance and acceptance of a formal challenge.

We warred against members of other tribes when they trespassed on our territory or raided. Killing Enemies, who weren't Persons, wasn't murder. It was defense of yourself and your band—defense of The People against evil beings whose souls weren't blessed by The Mother.

The People believed murder—any killing outside of legitimate challenge—was the ultimate crime. The only exception was when the survival of the band required it. Sometimes the old, the ill, or the crippled had to walk away or be ejected so the rest might survive. That had happened in our band last winter, but no one had been forced. Pressured, yes, but they weren't murdered. They agreed to leave. Nothing was done secretly. Only under the most extreme circumstances would Stone have forced them to go rather than persuaded them to do what was necessary. Under similar circumstances we sometimes put out babies who couldn't yet care for themselves. But they weren't People yet. Not until they were old enough to walk and talk and be ceremonially accepted into the band.

Any other killing of someone who hadn't been challenged, except in self-defense, was murder. Murder rarely happened among The People. I'd heard of only one instance in my lifetime. But when murder did occur, the murderer ceased being human, and thus became fair game for any revenge. And revenge wasn't an option. It was necessary. While a murderer remained among The People, the spirits would no longer bless us. We would experience hunger and disease and accidents. We believed we would continue suffering until the killer was punished or we, The People, were destroyed.

Down interpreted my silent thoughts as doubt. "Really. He was murdered. Someone stole Tall Pine's life."

I sighed. I'd scouted and returned with such important news. And suddenly it wasn't nearly as important. Not in the face of murder. It was hard to accept.

The last murder among The People took place when I was a boy, and so far away we only heard rumors of why it happened and how it was avenged. Most members of our band hadn't been alive then.

"What makes you call it murder?"

Down, Stone's daughter, was still a child, though barely. She was on the verge of womanhood, but hadn't yet bled. She was tall, slim, skinny almost, but with a hardness to her, a hidden strength I admired. She might never be as beautiful as Blue Flower, Stone's woman, but she was already pretty. And smart. I'd be willing to pay a fine dire wolf pelt for her when she came of age. Except Stone wasn't likely to accept it. He'd prevented me from having a woman for years. A man of the spirits should remain pure, he'd decided. Many of The People agreed. And he told the women that being associated with a Spirit Man was dangerous for them.

As far as I could tell, the spirits weren't in the least interested in whether I enjoyed the pleasures of the flesh. If they cared, why had they let me experience and enjoy them when I was young? I still yearned for a woman. And the spirits didn't seem to mind my occasional secret rendezvous.

One advantage of my age was that I had learned a great deal about how to please women. The women of our band knew that. A few risked encounters to share that pleasure. Others sought me out to learn how to give more to, and receive more from, their men—and how to better control them. My services might have been more popular if the men hadn't also heard those rumors about me. Most watched their women very carefully. A woman who cheated on her man couldn't be killed, but she could be beaten or disfigured. Even sent away from the band to survive on her own. And the man she cheated with was nearly always issued a formal challenge that was hard to refuse.

"We found a bowstring," Down said, "wrapped around his throat from behind."

I reached inside my tunic for the medicine pouch that hung from a thin leather string around my neck. It held a few herbs, a pinch of clay from the sacred place where I sought my first vision, some rocks with unique shapes and colors, pollen, and a crystal of great power.

"No. Not like that." She shook her head. "Bow sinew, pulled tight, like the garrote you made me. So tight it's buried in his flesh." She made a face, bugging out her eyes and letting her tongue loll from her open mouth. "Strangled."

I had to concentrate on how serious this was to keep from laughing. And I *had* made her a garrote. "You didn't…?"

She rolled her eyes. "Of course not. I'd have told you right away."

"Who killed him then?"

"That's what has my father so upset. No one knows. Gentle Breeze found the body when the old woman got up to stoke the morning fires. He was sprawled by the front of our tent, as if he'd been sitting beside the fire and someone came up behind him and…" She made the face again.

"What does Stone say?"

She shrugged. "You know my father. He's angry. Tall Pine was one of his favorites. He says the man who killed Tall Pine must pay the ultimate price. Someone has to know who did it and they'd better speak up. I think my father and Bull Hump and Takes Risks are all secretly afraid. But so far, all they've done is carry Tall Pine out of camp and down toward the lake." She nodded her head at a knob at the base of the ridge overlooking a small lake glowing golden in the afternoon sunlight. "They left him facing away from camp, of course, so his spirit won't see us in case it's looking for revenge."

That was as it should be. A dead person's spirit would always be angry. More so, a murdered one's. But that was only one of many things that needed to be done.

Stone's shout interrupted my thoughts. "Raven! You're finally back. Stop trying to seduce my child and get down here. We need you."

"It's not his fault," Down yelled back at her father. "I'm the one who's trying to seduce him."

She blushed with those bold words, though she stood beside me, straight and tall for everyone to see. She liked me well enough, but she'd be teased for this. She'd taken the sting out of it because of how she'd twisted her father's insult. Still, some people would take it seriously and ask what she wanted with such an old man. Did she hope an ancient like me might teach her sexual secrets so she could take many lovers? The boys and young men she was most likely attracted to were the ones who'd mock her most. And the girls near her age. I didn't envy her the taunting, but she could handle it.

"Our friend is dead," Stone told me. "We need a Spirit Man to bury him. That's you."

"Murdered!" I said into sudden silence. Our People's need to know had briefly overpowered their need to mourn. "If it's murder, I must find his killer."

Stone didn't respond. He probably had no idea how to solve any crime, let alone a murder. He knew brute force. It was the way he led. What I'd said was presumptuous. It should be his job, but I knew he'd be willing to leave this complicated task to me. If I succeeded, I might further prove my value to the band—above and beyond my ability to scout, hunt, heal, and intercede with the spirits. I'd demonstrate that my advice was worth hearing. That I could protect the band from enemies Stone couldn't even imagine. I didn't let myself think what might happen if I failed, or that I had no idea how to solve it either.

Before I started down the path toward the irregular cluster of tents, I pulled a short branch covered with waxy leaves out of my pack and handed it to Down. "Here's another plant for you to study. Don't eat it."

I brought her unusual plants to examine when I came back from scouting. Our band's healer, Gentle Breeze, was even older than I, and Down was the only person among us clever enough to assume the old woman's duties.

Down's eyes grew wide. "Is it poison?"

"No, but don't eat it. See if you can discover what its use might be. Tell me later. I'll be busy this afternoon."

"With Tall Pine's funeral. Can I help?"

"Not yet." At that moment I realized her skills might extend beyond healing into the realm of spirits. "And stop using the names of the dead, at least in front of anyone but me."

Down grinned and nodded. Her father shouted for me again. His patience was exhausted, and I obeyed.

◇◇◇

Our band had eleven tents. An unlucky number—one more than a man's fingers. Twelve was better—ten fingers and two feet. Or twenty, of course, if you counted toes instead. But there weren't many bands big enough to count toes. Luck was one reason I hoped to persuade Stone to take the mammoth. Another, because our camp was cramped and crowded. I was tired of lying in the dark, listening to Stone mount Blue Flower or Bull Hump rut with his two wives. I confess, it might not have bothered me so much if I'd had my own woman.

As I entered the confusion of the bereaved camp, I stopped and reassured Stone I'd do what must be done, and that I'd speak further with him and the other leaders shortly. Then I headed for the largest tent, the one I shared with Stone and Bull Hump and their families.

Stone didn't like me. He wasn't sure he believed I could actually read spirit signs or communicate with them. But he wasn't sure I couldn't. Either way, he saw me as a threat to him, and so he kept me close.

I went to release Snow. The dog howled when he saw me, and shuffled toward me wagging his great feathery tail. I dropped down and hugged him, untying the hobbles and leather rope Stone put on him to stop his following me when I left to scout. Snow, one of a dozen dogs in camp, was our best sentry. No stranger, no hungry bear, no rabid wolf, no one who wasn't a member of the band could come near without Snow's vigorous warnings. He'd been barking for me to let him loose since I arrived. But all the dogs were barking, joining their voices with the cries of the band. I'd only half freed Snow when he knocked me over and stood on my chest, welcoming me home with an eager face-washing. I wrestled with him until I removed the last bit of leather that secured him. Like a bolt, he shot across the tent and relieved himself on Stone's quiver. Not wise, but no one was there to see and I agreed with his opinion. He ran out then, looking for the other dogs or a ground squirrel to chase. I followed, to search among the wailing women.

There were two old women in our band. Gentle Breeze, who'd found Pine's body, and Scowl, born with a twisted face that made her look sullen and angry. Both were older than I, the only two people left in our band who were. Gentle Breeze had been my woman when we were very young. We had two sons. One died just after his birth. The other was killed by a wolf. Bad luck. I'd always suffered from it. Gentle Breeze and I weren't given another chance.

Bear Claw, Stone's father, traded one of his daughters to me for Gentle Breeze, who became his third woman. He wanted more sons and that was what she and I'd produced. But she gave him only daughters. After three, I might have had Gentle Breeze back. But Bear Claw's daughter, Willow, refused to share me with a second wife. Taking Gentle Breeze back might have lost me Willow. I lost her anyway, swept to her death as we crossed a swift river. I'd mourned her for many years, enough for Bear Claw to die and Stone to decide I shouldn't have a woman by the time I wanted one again. Almost twenty summers—too long.

Gentle Breeze and Scowl had followed the rituals, cutting themselves and rubbing ashes onto their skin and hair. The band had picked this campsite because it caught the wind and kept away mosquitoes and biting gnats. Not all, though, so wearing the ashes wouldn't be disagreeable.

I greeted them formally. "You found him," I said to Gentle Breeze. "So you're already unclean and must be purified."

She nodded. She'd never forgiven me for not taking her back when Bear Claw didn't want her anymore. I'd left her at risk—a single woman, one of the less necessary, except she'd become our healer, a mistress of herbs and poultices. I'd taught her then, as I was teaching Down now. Yet Gentle Breeze taught herself far more. So though I'd left her abandoned, I'd also introduced her to the profession that saved her. We remained friends, in our fashion, but our relationship was easy to strain.

"You know the rules of burial," I said. "You know what must be done. Until I can cleanse you and everyone in the band of the contamination from this crime, it's only logical for you to help me prepare his body."

Gentle Breeze agreed.

As I turned to Scowl, Snaggletooth—next to Snow the most dominant dog in our camp—danced around my feet, sniffing me. Like most of the dogs, he'd stopped barking when Snow reappeared. I ruffled Snaggletooth's ears.

"Yes, I know," Scowl grumbled. "I'm so old I'm practically dead already. Better to risk the victim's spirit vengeance on someone like me than a woman who can still bear children. And I know the rituals, too. Of course I'll help."

"Gather his things." I told them. "Get his women. Meet me at the main fire."

They went to do so.

Stone and Bull Hump and Takes Risks were tearing down the tent Tall Pine had shared with Takes Risks and their women and Tall Pine's children. Takes Risks had no children yet, or none who'd survived. They would bring me the tent so I might wash and purify it, making it harder for Tall Pine's soul to find it or harm the people who sheltered there. They'd set aside his tools and I picked among them, choosing the ones he'd find most useful in the world of the dead. I'd burn or discard what I didn't select—unless there was something Stone and his friends wanted to keep badly enough to accept the danger of doing so. Tall Pine would need what I picked when he went to live in the sky and built his hearth, another star among the countless fires that filled the night. Or had, when the sun set and we could still see them. That was another reason for concern. If Tall Pine couldn't find his way to the fires of the dead, he might try to remain with us. That was what Spirit Men had taught us for as long as I remembered. I taught the same message myself.

"Tell me about the one who died." I avoided Tall Pine's name. Stone and his friends would expect that.

Takes Risks shrugged. Bull Hump shook his head. Stone bit his lip as he considered what to say. The three were strong and cunning, but not deep thinkers.

"Gentle Breeze found him by the main fire," Takes Risks said. "He was strangled."

I already knew all that, of course, but it was my duty to ask. "Were there signs of a struggle?"

Stone looked south toward the shimmering mountains of ice, as if they might tell him the answer. "None that I saw."

"When Gentle Breeze found him, was it because the dogs barked? Did Snow sound the alarm?"

"No." Stone was stunned. He hadn't thought of that.

"Ah," I said.

"What?" Stone immediately regretted asking me. If someone else knew the right answer, he could pretend to have known it all along. Thought of it first, even.

"The killer must be one of us," I answered. "A member of our band."

◇◇◇

We buried Tall Pine in a small rock shelter near the top of the ridges above our camp. We couldn't dig a fitting hole for him, as we would have in the old country. Our options here were only ice or rock. If we dug into the tundra, we'd hit ice and find ourselves standing in a pool of freezing water too cold to work in for more than a few moments, making it impossible to dig deep enough. We couldn't dig on the ridges, either. Too much rock. I chose to put him in the rock shelter and cover him with more rocks. The women and I had a hard time of it, dragging him up to the spot and enlarging it. But what's necessary must be done.

When we finished the rituals, I sent the women down to the stream to wait for me to come purify them. We'd wash in the icy stream and then I'd dust us with pollen and brush away the danger with a grass whisk. But first, I must seal Pine's tomb.

I waited until the women were out of sight before I untied the bundle in which we'd wrapped Pine. I used a sharp stone blade to cut the bowstring out of his neck. The sinew wasn't fully cured, though it had proved tough enough for the job. It came from the elk we'd killed ten days ago. I'd left sinew bowstrings like this curing in Stone's tent. Most of the men in the band probably had them as well.

The string was tied at the ends to two pieces of wood. Not the tips of a bow—willow branches, fresh cut and green so they wouldn't snap, and thick so they wouldn't bend. I was surprised Stone hadn't noticed. Or had chosen not to mention it.

I recognized the garrote that killed him. I'd made it. Several days ago, Down had asked how to avoid the unwanted attentions of certain men. Men who thought all women wanted them and only resisted because it was expected. Having several extra bowstrings, thanks to the elk, I'd made her a garrote and taught her how to slip the cord around an assailant's throat while seeming to cooperate with his desires. I'd told her to be careful, of course. Not to squeeze it too tight. To immediately yell for help so the band could catch the criminal in the act and render a suitable punishment. But this garrote had been pulled so deep into Tall Pine's flesh that I doubted Down could have done it. It would have taken terrible anger, additional leverage, or someone very strong, like Stone or Bull Hump or Takes Risks.

I coiled the sinew and sticks and put them in my jerkin. Then I cut off the tip of Tall Pine's right thumb with my blade.

Tall Pine had been second in the band behind Stone—smarter and stronger, but not so ambitious. Still there'd been power in the man. I would burn away the flesh before it began to smell and save the bone. I'd keep it in my medicine pouch. Hears Voices, the old man who taught me how to listen to the spirits, told me there was much power to be gained by taking another's bones.

Much danger, too. I'd be cautious, but while I held part of Tall Pine, it was said I could bend his spirit to my bidding. I doubted that, but confronting his killer with this bone might be useful.

I spent the rest of the afternoon filling the mouth of Tall Pine's grave with rocks. It probably wouldn't matter. The scavengers would smell him, dig him out, feast on him. Yet his spirit would know I'd tried.

Thoroughly exhausted, I went through the rituals to purify us, then stumbled to my tent and Stone's. As I crawled into my sleeping robe, I realized I hadn't shared any of the news of what I'd discovered on scout. It was so important before I learned about the murder. Would the spirits let us take the pass to the south and The Earth Mother's promised land before we revenged Tall Pine's death? Would Stone and the other leaders agree to proceed before we found the killer and cleansed our band? If not, would we need the mammoth's flesh and a lucky twelfth tent? My eyes grew heavy wondering if anything mattered now but the murder.

Bone

I'd hardly closed my eyes before I no longer had eyes to close. No eyes at all, though I could "see" that I was in a strange hut. To my horror, a stranger held my bones in his hands. And strange is the right way to describe him.

His hair was short, but neatly tapered to varying lengths. I couldn't imagine how he'd gotten it to look that way. His beard and mustache were graying and likewise short, but they grew only around his upper lip, the corners of his mouth, and neatly down his chin. His cheeks were smooth and hairless.

He wore something faintly like a snow mask over his eyes. We cut slits in a strip of leather and wrap the masks over our eyes when bright sun turns the snow into frozen fire. Without those masks, a few hours' exposure can literally burn a man's eyes out and leave him forever blind. This man's mask was made of something like clear, thin ice surrounded by narrow dark bands that bridged his nose and disappeared behind his ears. They wouldn't hide his eyes from the sun. In fact, they made his eyes seem larger. He looked at me through this impossible mask and said, "I don't think our friend is happy with his fate."

He couldn't begin to imagine. My bones in his hands...?

He spoke a language I'd never heard, yet I caught the meaning and understood him.

Another voice spoke. A woman's. I didn't understand her at all, but I had at least a sense of what she said because he understood her.

"Put him down. We need to talk."

He glanced from me to her. His eyes were the palest I'd ever seen.

"You should learn patience, like our friend here. I'd say he's spent at least fifteen thousand years waiting to tell us his story."

The number astounded me. It took me a moment to comprehend because The People arrived at large numbers by multiplying tens. I had no time to consider the meaning of such a vast sum because he began bouncing me in his hand. Then he turned me to face the woman.

I'd thought Blue Flower was beautiful. This woman was... perfect. Flawless as a child and yet with the full curves of womanhood. Amazing curves, all perfect. Too perfect. And the skins she wore...they were as perfect as she, and dyed in colors I'd never seen. Once, I'd come across a flower of a similar hue to the leathers that clung to her amazing breasts, but it hadn't been nearly as bright. The clothing clung to her without wrinkles, seams, or stitches.

"Your woman suspects that I'm not just overseeing your work," the perfect one said, "so she's going to make you choose between us."

Woman wasn't quite the word she used. She meant something more formal but I had no way to express it. I found it hard to imagine a woman being in charge of a man's work. But none of this made any sense.

"Look at his teeth," the one with ice eyes said. "Remarkable condition but see the wear? How old do you suppose he might have been?"

The woman touched her skins. They fell away and shocked me yet again. Her sex was as hairless as a pre-adolescent's, and yet her shape was very much that of a woman. Her breasts were full and incredibly upright for their size. Unlike any I'd ever seen. Her waist was slender, taut with muscles. Her navel had been pierced with something that gleamed.

"When she makes you choose, ask yourself if she can give you this." The perfect woman removed me from his hand and put me on a flat slab of wood. I could see them no more. Instead, a world filled with exact angles and incredibly smooth surfaces lay in front of me. The place was brightly lit by strips of fire that burned white-hot along the roof of this astounding hut. Yet they produced only light and did no damage. Amazing!

I heard noises below the slab on which she'd put me. At first, I didn't understand. Then I recognized them. Sounds like that had kept me awake and frustrated in Stone's tent. Imagining how the perfect woman looked as they made those sounds should have held my interest. Except I suddenly realized my head rested on the wood with no room for more of me below. The rest of me was missing. I wasn't bones. I was only skull.

◇◇◇

I bolted awake, drenched in cold sweat. Around me, others in Stone's tent slept the sleep of exhaustion. I felt at least as done in by yesterday's events, but I knew I wouldn't sleep again. I scrambled out of my bedding, still in my leathers. As I fumbled my way into my boots, my right hip complained. There was a sore spot, as if I'd foolishly made my bed without clearing away all the rocks that lay underneath. I pushed my robes and some grass padding aside. There was no rock. Instead, I uncovered a crude doll, a human figure formed of willow twigs tied with strips of leather. The knot that tied them was peculiar, unlike any I'd seen before.

Even though I'm not convinced of the existence of the spirits I serve, or their interest in our daily lives, I reacted with a shiver. A doll could be an innocent child's toy. But not this one. Its head had been soaked in blood—dry now. Someone had used it to cast a spell on me. Could having the head covered in blood have something to do with my dream of being a skull?

I slipped quietly out of the tent flap, disturbing no one. The sun had only begun rising along its summer circle of this northern sky. Our central fire still glowed in its pit. I tossed the doll on the coals and watched it begin to burn. I spoke the words, sprinkled a little pollen, and brushed myself clean with a grass whisk. The doll blazed, quickly gone.

I took the trail that led down to the stream. I'd wash myself clean of the dream and start this day fresh. I'd cleanse my body, then more fully purify my soul with the spirits again, just in case.

Before I reached the stream, I paused. I'd heard a quiet coughing in the willows. I should have brought my spear and bow. There wasn't time to go back for them. I picked up a heavy stone, suitable for throwing, and slipped into the thicket.

I heard the sound again. Clearer, this time. I recognized it. I pushed aside enough branches to confirmed my suspicion. She was bent over, vomiting in the scraggly grass.

"I told you not to eat it." I dropped the rock and stepped into the little clearing.

Down swung in my direction, wiping her mouth but grinning in pleased surprise.

"I didn't. Well, only a tiny bit just after I got up. The plant, it's to purge someone of a poison they ate, right? Or of meat gone bad."

"Obviously," I said. "But why eat it yourself?"

"If I'm going to use this to treat anyone else, I have to understand just how it will affect them. What healer would fail to know the consequences of the cure she prescribed?"

"Clever girl," Gentle Breeze agreed, slipping through the willows behind me.

Down smiled again. "I thought this might be an agent to purge someone's stomach. That's why I only tasted a little. I didn't manage to try it yesterday because of all the excitement. So I woke early and came down here into the willows to test it."

"Good for you, Down," Gentle Breeze said. "Between Raven and me, we'll turn you into an amazing healer. But right now, I need to speak to Raven in private."

"I'll go wash my mouth out in the stream," Down said. "Your plant left a bitter taste."

As soon as the girl was gone I apologized. "I hope you don't mind that I'm also teaching the girl. Do you think she'd be interested in learning about the spirits, too? You and I are getting old and there's no one else in the band smart enough to take our places."

"It's a good idea," Gentle Breeze said. "But that's not what I want to talk to you about."

I raised an eyebrow in question while she sorted through her pouch.

"I couldn't get you alone yesterday, but you need to know about this. Look what I found on the chest of the one who was murdered."

She pulled out a doll like the one I'd found this morning and handed it to me. There was no blood on this one. Its crude arms had been tied so they bent across its chest and held a small yellow wildflower.

"Does anyone else know about this?" I said.

She shook her head.

"Let's keep it that way for now."

I took the doll apart, undoing the same strange knots, then led her to the stream. I purified the pieces before I let them float away. Then I purified both of us.

"Bad enough that we have a murderer among us," Gentle Breeze said. "Worse to have a witch."

Hunt

The mammoth had moved upstream from where I first saw her. A pack of wolves had been at her and she bled from fresh wounds. The crushed corpses of two pack members showed she was still capable of defending herself.

Because of the wolves, perhaps, she'd climbed to a shelf a man's height above the river. The water skirted the foot of a solitary mountain there. Great slabs of gray rock sprinkled with red and orange and gold lichens stood out from the soil to support the earth's grasp for the sky. The mammoth cow had placed her back against one and limited the ability of the wolves to get at her hindquarters. It would limit us, as well.

We'd taken four days to get there, though I'd traveled the same distance in less than one. Moving the band was always slow, but we'd wasted time while Stone and his seconds bickered and slowed our journey. Tall Pine had them scared. Everyone was afraid. The murder obsessed us all, made us suspicious. Stone and Bull Hump and Takes Risks kept together, covering each other's backs. They were our leaders, as Tall Pine had been. That might mean they were most at risk. They thought so.

I finally persuaded Stone we couldn't stay where we were until the crime was solved. With Tall Pine's corpse just above us on the ridge, staying made it far too easy for his angry spirit to find us. We'd be safer heading for the passage between the glaciers I'd found. On the way we could guarantee we had plenty to eat—to say nothing of increasing our luck by adding a twelfth tent.

I'd said I would discover the murderer, so I circulated among the band and asked people where they were the night Tall Pine died. I spoke to those who shared tents. No one had left a tent that night, I was told. But sneaking in and out of tents while others slept was easy and common. I asked Down if she still had her garrote. She couldn't find it. That troubled me, but I didn't believe she was strong enough to have pulled the cord so deep into Tall Pine's throat. I believed her when she denied killing him.

I looked for dolls, and listened for word of people finding them. If anyone else in the band had been a victim of witchcraft, I heard nothing of it.

I searched through people's belongings when no one watched me. I asked everyone what they might have heard, both that night and in discussion within the band. Who did they think might be guilty? I watched to see who acted abnormally. That didn't help because no one acted normally. Why would they, when one of us had just been murdered? I particularly watched Stone and Bull Hump and Takes Risks, and enjoyed it because my watching made them uncomfortable. But I didn't learn anything I hadn't already known.

It snowed one afternoon. Then the sun broke through and turned the tundra so bright that we strapped on our snow masks. That was the first I'd thought of my terrible dream since the morning I woke from it. I shivered, not from the cold. But then I wiped the dream from my mind again. I'd slept since. Dreamed again, without more visits from the stranger or the perfect woman. It was odd that I'd dreamed myself a skull. I'd never heard of anyone dreaming something like that. But I'd destroyed the doll from my bedding as well as the one Gentle Breeze found. And I'd done what I could to protect us all from witchcraft. The dream must have been a peculiar nightmare that wouldn't happen again.

The snow had melted by the time we reached the mammoth. Burned off but for a few patches high up the mountain's side where dall sheep grazed.

While the women set up camp on an island in mid-stream, Stone led our hunters to the mammoth. Much of the hair about the old cow's face and shoulders had gone gray. One of her tusks had broken in some long-ago battle. So long, that the shorter tusk was nearly smooth on the end. Her right rear leg still supported no weight. I was surprised she'd managed to climb the ledge, though wolves provided ample encouragement.

For the first time in days, the band felt comfortable to me. We had food to gather. Danger to face. We were about to do something that required all of us to play roles we knew. Tall Pine's murder became secondary to taking the mammoth.

The wolves didn't challenge us as we approached. They simply melted away like yesterday's snow, hurried a little by our dogs. We were too few to take all the meat the cow carried. It was as if the wolves decided to let us suffer the danger and losses, then satisfy themselves on our leavings. It struck me as a wise strategy.

Stone and Bull Hump and Takes Risks looked the cow over and then gathered apart from the rest of us to decide how to take her. While they did, we gathered the dogs and tied them so they wouldn't try to help us and get themselves killed for their trouble. Then all the adult men stripped down to our breechclouts, left our belongings in neat piles, and took up our spears and atlatls and our bows and arrows.

I walked forward and stopped in front of the mammoth. Dangerously close if she still had the use of all four legs. She watched me through ancient bloodshot eyes, weary but angry. I spoke to her.

"I apologize for what we are about to do to you. Though it's a kindness, really. You'll suffer less from us than from the wolves. Even if you drive us away, your days will be numbered and miserable. We appreciate what you'll give us. Full bellies on which we may make a long journey, and your hide for a new tent. We'll carve wonders from your precious ivory—tools and carvings that will be appreciated for generations. You'll join the Spirit of the Mammoths and The Earth Mother in the sky pastures until you're reborn and given back your youth. You'll be a ruler of the tundra again, so great and powerful you need fear no other creature."

I didn't mention that she'd have to grow old again. It was time to celebrate what she'd been and would be again. Not remind her of endings.

She grumbled at me and rocked back and forth on her forelegs, as if impatient to get on with it. I could see that, while she might agree with my logic, she'd give us another gift as well. The gift of resistance. She intended to teach us how to fight for life because it was precious. If she must die, she'd show us how to die well.

"See how she watches Raven," Stone called. "Fan out along her right side from Raven to the wall of stone. Make noise. Keep her attention." Stone stepped over and tapped Hair on Fire, handing the young man our sacred spear—the mammoth killer. Hair on Fire smiled and nodded and hugged the edge of the ledge as he circled around to the beast's left. Did I see someone above and behind him for a moment? One of the wolves, probably. Or my imagination. All the men were where they should be.

Hair on Fire? I hadn't expected him. Usually, it would be an experienced hunter, one of the leaders. Stone or Bull Hump or Takes Risks or, until four days ago, Tall Pine. Hair on Fire was a surprising choice. He was young, but strong and quick. His confidence growing. He'd asked Stone for the right to a woman of his own a few months ago. That was when Slender Reed came of age and everyone knew the young couple wanted each other. She was beautiful, except for the scar a fox had given her when she was a child. The scar hadn't spoiled her body though. There was promise in her youthful curves. But Stone gave Slender Reed to Tall Pine, instead. Tall Pine already had a woman, one he shared with the rest of the leaders.

The sharing of women by our leaders was something that was both known and not known. Not known, because it ran contrary to The People's laws. Not known, because Blue Flower refused to be shared, and refused, also, to allow Stone to share those other women. The People believed a woman was worthy of having such wishes honored. Or, at least, not having them openly violated. Stone continued in the sharing, but he'd been careful about it and, though Blue Flower probably knew, she could pretend otherwise.

Also known, but not known, was a rumor that Hair on Fire and Slender Reed still met in the willows from time to time, including shortly before Tall Pine's murder. Stone might have decided that made Fire a suspect. Did that explain the young man being put in this hunt's most dangerous position? If so, Stone should have discussed his suspicions with me. Giving Fire the honor of killing the mammoth could prove dangerous to Stone's leadership. Hair on Fire was popular, especially among the young men. If he killed the mammoth, his prestige would soar. If he was a threat to Stone and his friends now, he'd be more so after that. He'd be a champion to the disaffected among us and a hero to the rest of the young men, especially those also impatiently waiting for women of their own. Could Stone and Bull Hump and Takes Risks have a plan to insure Fire would fail? Or was it that they simply couldn't imagine him being capable of killing the cow?

For The People, killing a mammoth is an exceptional event. The simplest way requires being in the right place at the right time. Near a convenient cliff surrounded by dry grass with the wind blowing in the right direction. Occasionally, mammoths can be panicked by fire and driven over a cliff, dying from the fall. Not often. Mammoths are among the wisest of beasts. Unless the cliff is all but undetectable until the last moment or the fire is extreme enough, they'll stop, turn, even charge back through flames that cause painful burns. They're seldom deterred if men stand in their way shooting arrows and waving robes at them. Not even if those men are accompanied by dogs.

The most common method of killing a mammoth is to bleed it to death. The band's hunters attack in mass, hurling spears with their atlatls, shooting arrows, doing as much damage as possible and then scampering away…if they're lucky. Most hunts of this sort result in the death of several dogs and at least one hunter.

Or serious injuries, especially if we try to cut a single mammoth out of a herd. But once a beast is injured badly enough, it's only a matter of time. It will grow increasingly weak and, eventually, lie down and die or hardly resist the quicker end we bring it. This, without our active participation, was our situation.

We had a ledge here, but it was too low for a fall to kill the cow, even if we could somehow drive her over its edge. But because she was already hurt, weakened, and alone, we could try a quicker method. Quicker, and more dangerous.

All of us would keep her attention while Hair on Fire came at her from downwind. When he got close enough, we would make as much noise as possible and attack together. Except for the dogs, though they'd bark and growl from where they'd been tied and help us focus the cow's mind. We'd make the cow hurt enough to want to hurt us back. Then, while her attention was fully occupied, Fire would rush in and get beneath her. He'd thrust the short, stout spear with our sharpest obsidian tip up through her belly. He'd aim just below the bottom of her rib cage and drive it straight to her heart. If Fire's luck held, he'd scramble out from under the mammoth before she collapsed on him or, if the spear hadn't been properly aimed, before the cow caught him as he ran away.

Hair on Fire had disappeared into the rocks and brush, downwind, on the old cow's left side. When he got as close to her as the cover allowed, he crawled out to a spot where I could see him. He waved. I passed the signal along to the rest of the men. We went at her, whooping and whistling and hurling rocks. A few waved skin robes. The mammoth kept her back to the stone and nodded her great head from side to side, keeping one eye in Fire's direction and the other on us. This one had faced men before.

"Now!" Stone yelled. As one, we charged her. We threw spears. With the leverage of our atlatls most drove deep into her flesh. We shot arrows. They did little more than sting her, but they held her attention. Snaggletooth got free of the ropes that tied the rest of the dogs. He rushed in and snapped at her mighty legs. She caught him with a tusk and threw him back among us, bruised but not seriously hurt.

Hair on Fire rose from where he lay and ran at her. At the last second, the cow turned, not toward us as she was supposed to, but back toward Fire. Instead of breaking off his attack, Fire tried to slip between the cow's side and the stone wall. The mammoth swung her head and the broken stump of her left tusk caught the boy and rammed him face-first into the rock. The band's mammoth-killing spear clattered to the surface of the ledge under the cow. She seized the boy with her trunk and threw him against the wall again. Our spears and arrows had hurt the cow, but not nearly enough. The beast had turned so she faced away from most of us. She was sideways to me, where I stood at the far end of our line. She pummeled Fire, dashing him against the rocks and bringing her good tusk to savage the boy's body.

I stopped thinking. I dropped my bow and ran under the cow. I scooped up the short spear, found the spot just beneath where the last of her ribs joined, and, with everything I had, drove the point up toward her heart. She screamed. I threw myself against the stone wall. If I'd hurt her badly, she should fall the other way toward her injured leg, and not where I crouched against the stone. If I'd failed, the monster would transfer her attentions from the boy to me.

I heard the cow cry a second time as I reached the rock. Rage and agony echoed in her voice. Her head turned away from Fire and her eyes found me. I reached out and grabbed the boy's arm. I pulled him toward me and his body streaked the rocks with gore. The cow's eyes glistened with acceptance and began to cloud. She toppled away from me. Her fall shook the earth.

Discoveries

I carried Hair on Fire down from the ledge. His head had lost its shape. He was unrecognizable. Even the unusual tint of his hair hardly showed through all the blood he'd lost. He'd been named for the way his hair glowed in the sun, and for his lightning-quick mood changes.

Down caught me from behind as I waded toward the island. The rest of the women and children waited there, so she took me by surprise. She nearly knocked me over as she tried to tear his body from my grasp. She howled with real grief, not formal mourning. Her face streamed with tears. Her nails scratched me before the other women rushed over and pulled her away.

I knew Down was attracted to Fire. What young woman in our band wouldn't have been? But I hadn't realized the depth of her feelings. She'd hidden them well—until now.

An immense task lay before us. We'd killed a mammoth. Skinning and butchering it would take at least the rest of the day. Then as much meat as we could gather had to be cooked or smoked.

We'd lost a band member, too. He must be purified and mourned. His corpse had to be prepared and buried right away, before his spirit returned, angry at our failure to draw the mammoth from him.

To complicate matters, Bull Hump had taken an arrow in the neck. One of us had shot wildly in the confusion. Or, worse, maybe one of us hadn't quite shot accurately. I'd seen Stone pull the arrow from Bull Hump, and heard our Bull's wounded bellow. I'd heard, too, Takes Risks wondering if the shot had been an accident. Normally, I'd have joined that discussion while treating Bull Hump's wound at least until Gentle Breeze could see to him. If someone had tried to kill our mighty Bull Hump, then Takes Risks and Stone were definitely targets—our band's leadership. Not likeable men. Not especially capable men, though the band had prospered most of the time in spite of their deficiencies and the difficulty of our journey.

Things had gone better for us since last winter. This land was rich with game. We'd collected abundant berries and edible roots, shoots, and leaves after spring returned, and so we'd traveled a long way with few hardships. No disasters, until Tall Pine and now Hair on Fire. And the wounding of Bull Hump. Until the last few days, our lives had been good enough so even poor leadership would normally go unchallenged. Murder changed that. And murder wasn't a normal tool for switching leaders.

We were going to be very busy that day. The first of many. Just as well, I thought, that the sun only circled the sky here and our days had turned perpetual. I had no idea when I might sleep again.

◇◇◇

We cried in the wilderness. We wailed while some skinned the mammoth with sharp blades and began to scrape its hide. We mourned as others butchered the carcass. We wept while we gathered dry wood and animal dung from this nearly treeless land so we could preserve the meat. We shed tears while Bull Hump's wound was treated and as I carried Hair on Fire downstream to wash the blood off him and pray over his body.

The mourning continued when I made my way back to camp for Fire's possessions and to find women to help me wrap and stitch him in his skins. Women who'd also help me find and prepare a place to leave his body, then carry it there. Gentle Breeze and Scowl, I'd hoped, previous companions in too many burials and, therefore, ones who knew their roles.

Gentle Breeze still treated the wound at the base of Bull Hump's neck. From the way he fought her efforts and complained how terribly she hurt him with every touch, I knew he wasn't badly injured. But he'd keep her busy answering his complaints longer than I could afford to wait.

Stone stopped me as I crossed our temporary camp. "Where are your arrows?"

I shrugged. "I shot them all. Or most. Actually, I think a couple were still in my quiver when I dropped my bow and ran to grab the spear."

He showed me an arrow, its tip still bloody. "Is this yours?"

The shaft was straight, the arrowhead sharp with skillfully knapped flint. The fletching was well done, too. I preferred duck feathers for mine. These were ptarmigan.

I ignored the implication in his question. "Is this the arrow that wounded Bull Hump?" I twirled it in my fingers. It hadn't been decorated and I mentioned that to Stone. "It's a plain hunting arrow. A good one, but nearly any of us could have made it."

"It's not yours?" From his tone, I knew he wanted me to claim the arrow and thus solve his problem of who shot Bull Hump.

"Go look for my quiver. It'll be at the end of the line. You and Bull Hump were only a few paces from me. If I'd shot in your direction, I'd have nearly taken the nose off the man next to me. Ask him where my arrows went. Besides, you know I fletch my arrows with duck feathers and mark them by carving a raven's claw. That's what you'll find in my quiver."

He knew, but my answers weren't the ones he wanted. He thought for a moment. Thinking didn't come easy for Stone. "This arrow matches no one's. The few who use ptarmigan feathers are all young men. Their arrows are much cruder than this, and they usually paint complex designs on them."

"So it's likely," I said, "that whoever shot Bull Hump did it on purpose."

From the way Stone raised his eyebrows I could tell he agreed, but hadn't followed my reasoning.

"The arrow is disguised," I said. "Plain. Not like any our hunters shot at the mammoth, right?"

He nodded.

"So it wasn't meant for the beast. It was meant for Bull Hump."

"Or me," Stone said. "It whistled past my ear."

"Or you," I agreed.

"Shit." He turned away, probably to go search my quiver.

◇◇◇

I found Scowl and Down together. The old woman held Down in her arms and comforted her while a cluster of girls hung around. The girls were young, only one of them, Slender Reed, old enough to have bled, and that just for a few moons. They wailed their own laments instead of helping soothe Down. Even Slender Reed didn't seem as upset as Down.

"Take your grieving elsewhere." I shooed them away. As they went I suddenly realized how much shorter than Down all of them were. The years fly past for the old, like Scowl and me. We lose track, especially of children. How old was Down? When I did the calculations I realized this was her sixteenth summer. That was late for a woman to come of age. It usually happened by fourteen. Very few girls failed to bleed until their sixteenth year. In fact, I realized, none of the girls I'd just sent away were more than fourteen, not even Slender Reed. Our band had several women younger than Down already raising babies.

"I need help with the burial," I told Scowl.

She gestured at Down. "I don't want to leave her in the care of those children."

I put a hand on Down's shoulder. "You touched him as I carried him across the river. So you also must be purified. Will you help me bury him?"

Down continued to sob, not answering.

I had to have help. The sun had already passed its high point. Hair on Fire should be in his grave before another day began. There was so much else to do. So I slapped Down. The blow was louder than it was hard. In my experience, slapping a hysterical woman is likely to make things worse, not better, but I was desperate. To my surprise, it shocked Down enough for me to get her attention.

"You cared for him." I didn't make it a question. "If you care enough, there's only one way to do anything for him now."

Her eyes were swollen with tears, but they looked into mine. "What?" she hiccupped, her voice ragged.

"He must be made ready and then buried. Some preparations require things only his woman can do." I dropped my voice to a whisper and bent to put my mouth by her ear. "Stone gave him no woman. Perhaps he picked his own. Or you picked him. It doesn't matter. If you care for him, I need your help."

She drew an arm across her eyes in an effort to wipe away the tears.

"Tell me what to do."

I stood and spoke in a normal voice so Scowl could hear. "I want you to go with Scowl. Help gather his things. Choose those that were most precious to him. Meet me downstream where the island ends. Scowl will tell you what else to bring."

"All right," she said. "I'll do as you ask."

◇◇◇

I did what I could to make Hair on Fire presentable. After I washed him, I pushed the broken bones in his head around enough to make him recognizable. It helped, but his face remained too flat and his features too twisted.

I washed and hastily purified myself from the mammoth slaying. I had managed to sip a bit of the old cow's blood and thanked her for it. I'd slit her throat to free her soul. But I should have gotten water from the stream and poured it in her mouth—a last drink before she made her spirit journey and went to live among the stars in the company of The Earth Mother. I hadn't had the time, so as I prepared the boy's corpse I spoke to the cow's memory. Then I cleansed myself in the icy water and brushed the beast's death from my body with a grass whisk and a pinch of pollen from my medicine pouch.

Down stopped in her tracks the moment she entered the clearing and saw the boy. She dropped the things she carried and began trembling. I thought she might fall and I ran to her, grabbed her by the arms, and turned her face away from him.

"Down, you can mourn him for the rest of your life. Right now, you owe him more. Do you understand?"

She agreed, though the tears came again and I knew it was all she could do to contain her sobs.

Scowl stood and watched, puzzled. "Give me a moment with the girl," I told the old woman. "Let me calm her. Wait by the body."

Scowl didn't argue. She'd helped me with burials often. She wanted to be finished with the job. Her own would come all too soon. She'd rather live the days she had left without reminders of what awaited her.

When the old woman was out of earshot, I spoke to Down again. "I need you to be honest with me. It's forbidden for a child to be a woman to a man, but you've been a woman to the man the mammoth killed, haven't you? You lay with him."

She pulled herself together, threw her shoulders back and faced me without shame. I expected no less.

"I've been Fire's woman, but I'm no child. I had my first bleeding three moons ago."

"You shouldn't speak his name."

"Why not? You don't hesitate to speak the names of the dead."

She was clever, this one. Clever enough to hide her bleeding from the band. And fearless enough to admit it to me.

"Have you lain with others?" I asked. "And what about Slender Reed? I've heard the two of them enjoyed each other's company even after she became Tall Pine's woman."

Not that either question mattered at the moment. Except to me, because I needed to trust her if I planned to continue helping her become our next healer, and possibly, my apprentice.

"No," she said. "I haven't lain with other men. As I grew up, I touched boys and they touched me, but you know all the children do that. As for Slender Reed...of course that troubled me, but I thought I could make him like me better. I hoped he'd decide to be my man."

"Becoming an adult gives you new rights and responsibilities. Why did you hide it?"

"After my father gave Slender Reed to Tall Pine instead of Fire, I decided I wanted Fire for myself. So I asked my father to let me have Fire as soon as my time came. My time was just beginning then, but I hid it in case Stone refused. That's what he did. He told me my choice might weaken his ability to remain headman of our band. He said he'd give me to someone who supported or strengthened him, or maybe someone from another band. If he traded me for another band's woman, some stranger, he'd give her to Fire. My father thought the band would take a long time accepting a new woman, one they didn't already know, and that might offset Fire's popularity. I told him what I thought of the idea and he threatened to just give me to Walks Like Ox."

Walks Like Ox was well named. Big, slow, dull, very strong, and a little cruel. I understood why Down's reaction to the prospect had been dismay. The threat of being traded and becoming a stranger in a strange band wouldn't have appealed either.

"You hid the bleeding? You mixed with men, touched their belongings and food while you were unclean?"

Any other woman would have averted her eyes with shame at such an accusation. Down met my stare.

"I did," she said. "I thought I could make my father change his mind, especially if I could persuade Fire to offer a generous gift for me."

I wasn't as angry as I pretended, though nearly all our band would be outraged. I wasn't frightened because I served whatever spirits might exist. I knew protections in case the spirits actually cared what we'd done. And, I confess, there'd been times when I so needed a woman that her bleeding hadn't prevented our coupling. Even that threat to my manhood hadn't deterred me. Those acts caused me no harm. Of course, I'd never become a leader. None of my children had survived. Perhaps such things were my punishments or, more likely, I was simply unlucky.

On the day Fire died, it had been so long since I'd had a woman that bleeding wouldn't have stopped me. But the band must never know I'd violated that taboo and would be willing to do so again. Even more, they must never know what Down had done. They might judge Down's contamination as the cause of Fire's death. In fact, they could blame the murder on her acts. Then, even though I'd purify them, and even with Stone as her father, they might drive her away—send her onto the tundra alone and unarmed.

If they did that, I wondered if I'd offer to go with her...and if she'd have me.

"How did you manage to hide it?" How would a child like Down—a child just becoming a woman—know what to do to disguise her condition?

Down turned her face away. "Someone helped. I won't tell you who. I told her about Fire and Walks Like Ox. She said a woman should have the same right as a man to decide who she couples with. She said there were ways to hide my condition. Plants, herbs. Dressings I must secretly wash and change. And ways to avoid having a child."

"Gentle Breeze." Who else? Down's mother had died the year after bearing her. Stone's woman, Blue Flower, didn't like Down. Down was much smarter than Blue Flower and they were nearly the same age. It had to be Gentle Breeze. I'd coupled with Gentle Breeze when she bled, I remembered, back when she was my woman. And on occasions, after that.

"No, not Gentle Breeze," Down said. "I can't tell you who." She wouldn't meet my eyes as she said it.

Of course it was Gentle Breeze. But that didn't matter. "Don't ever tell anyone else. Not about Gentle Breeze. Not about Hair on Fire. And most especially, not about hiding your bleeding. Imagine how the band might punish you."

"Not so badly as you think, Raven. I'm not the first girl to hide her bleeding in order to be available to the man she wanted."

That took me aback.

Down must have seen it on my face. "I thought our Spirit Man knew everything."

"No," I confessed. "About some things I'm just an old fool."

"I was sure you knew. And that you knew I'd become a woman. I thought that was why you were paying me so much attention lately. I was flattered."

I didn't know what to say to that, and then another problem struck me. "Are you bleeding now?"

Men didn't ask women such things. When her time came, a woman simply packed what she needed and went to stay in our Women's tent. Only other women could enter there for their own bleeding, to bear children, or to visit those who stayed there while they were unclean. Residents of the Women's tent spoke to no man, met no man's eye, touched no tools except women's tools which had to be cleansed and purified before being used by anyone else. Even visitors had to wash and ritually purify themselves before reentering the main camp and coming in contact with men.

"No," Down said. "I'm not bleeding now."

"When your next bleeding comes, it will be your first. Be certain Blue Flower knows when it happens. As soon as you're through, Stone will host a great celebration of your womanhood."

"And give me to Walks Like Ox."

"No. Ox won't get you."

"Why not? Will you stop him?"

"Trust me."

I didn't know how, but I'd find a way. Ox didn't deserve someone as precious as Down. I wouldn't mind having her for myself, though I had no more idea how to arrange that than how to keep her from Ox. Not yet, anyway.

When she looked in my eyes, I saw she did trust me. I hoped I'd prove worthy. I'd certainly try.

"Down, prepare yourself. We must act for our dead. Come, do exactly as Scowl and I tell you. When we've put him in his grave, I'll send you and Scowl to wait until I purify all of us before we return to camp. But you'll slip away from Scowl and sneak back to the grave. There are things a woman should do for her man to free his soul so it will be at peace and move on."

"What things?" Acting as Hair on Fire's woman strengthened her.

"A woman should caress her man's genitals one last time before they're washed and purified. A hair from between her legs should be left with him, that he may carry her sex to the spirit world and not need to come in search of it here. That's all."

"I plucked those hairs so no one would see them and know I've become a woman."

I rolled my eyes. She'd gone to a great deal of trouble for Fire. I hoped he'd been worth it. And I wished some woman felt that strongly about me.

"Perhaps a few have grown in since."

"I can check."

I remembered the hairless sex of the perfect woman in my dream. I wondered whether Down needed help searching for such a hair. The timing of my thoughts and the stirring that accompanied them couldn't have been more inappropriate. I turned and focused on Fire's battered corpse. The thoughts and stirring subsided.

"Come help Scowl and me now. Your friend deserves the best we can give him."

◇◇◇

It was a long day. Two days, actually. I only realized we'd begun the second when we lost the sun behind the mountain.

Down had rejoined me at the rock shelter I'd discovered on the stream's side of the peak by then. She hadn't needed to sneak away from Scowl. When they reached the river to wait for me, Scowl felt exhausted and took a nap among the willows. Down had hurried back to perform her duties for her man, acting with a gentle fondness that made me jealous. And she found new hair between her legs. Several, all plucked for Fire's pleasure and without my help. I didn't offer. She was young and in love for the first time. It ended tragically. I remembered my first lover. I've always remembered. Sex first shared is special. I'd loved other women more, and more skillfully but memories of that first time remained precious. Down's newfound sexuality combined with her youth and innocence reminded me of what that felt like. I longed to offer her comfort, but she had no need of a suitor just then. My age let me understand that.

She cried giving him his final caress, and came into my arms for reassurance. I held her until I began to feel aroused. Then I put her to work, helping me fill the chamber in which he lay. Stacking the rocks was hard work. She felt useful focusing her mind on the task instead of on her loss. If Scowl should wake and notice Down was gone, I told her to say she'd taken a walk in the willows. Doing so would have been foolish, but the young do foolish things.

There was bear scat on the stony slope below the rock shelter. In this country, rock shelters were about the only place we could use for burials. But they weren't secure. This one certainly wouldn't be. I'd removed a few bones and other evidence that a bear had used this place from time to time. A big grizzly, I thought from the scat's size. If Down saw evidence of the bear, she ignored it. We piled layers of rocks over her lover, maybe enough to deter the animal, especially if it caught wind of the mammoth carcass down below. Of course, the bear would have to contest the wolves for that meat, but wolves might be less trouble than the rocks Down and I moved.

After I purified Scowl and Down and myself because of our direct contact with the dead, I joined the men bringing firewood to cure and cook the meat we'd butchered. Scowl and Dawn got scrapers and worked helping the women clean flesh from the mammoth's hide. We wouldn't have time to cure it properly. We'd have a new tent by the time we next pitched camp again, big enough to relieve our crowding, but pungent.

Boys who weren't yet men kept the fires burning under the strips of meat we'd hung from green willows. We found dry wood and dung to feed those fires. We had taken enough meat to provide for the band for at least a moon.

The sun had worked his way around from behind the mountain again by the time I left the boys to their task and went to Stone's tent. Stone slept. Bull Hump slept. So did a few others. I crawled into my own bedding and tried not to let the comings and goings of others disturb me. I must have been successful. I woke and the light was brighter outside. Stone stood over me, frowning. I wasn't sure why, at first. Then I realized Down had crawled into my arms while I lay sleeping.

"She should have come to you for comfort," I told him.

"She did. I told her she was too old for such nonsense."

"Not today."

He scowled at me, but he left.

Maybe I only dreamed that. Down was gone when I woke again and Stone never mentioned the incident. Neither did anyone else. And again, my dreams were normal enough—death, blood, the mammoth, and the feel of Down in my arms. Not of the ice-eyed stranger who'd found my skull.

Trial

The camp echoed with chaos and shouting when I next woke. Bull Hump's booming roar rose over a chorus of angry voices, so many I couldn't make out what they said. I rolled out of my robes, struggled into my boots, grabbed my spear, and went to see.

Bull Hump, Stone, and Takes Risks formed a half circle around Walks Like Ox and a pair of his friends. They all shouted at each other.

I saw Ox every day, but I was surprised at how big he'd grown. He was bigger even than Bull Hump. Softer, maybe, but Bull Hump had just taken an arrow in the neck. Even in his rage, Bull Hump held his head at an angle to ease the pain. Gentle Breeze had made him a poultice for the wound, but the skin around it was red and swollen.

I leaned my spear against our tent when I saw we weren't under attack. Ours wasn't the only tribe crossing the tundra. Occasionally, quarrels broke out between bands within The People. Stone had thought the price asked for Blue Flower was too high, so he'd never finished paying it. That was two summers ago. We still heard rumors that Blue Flower's band intended, one way or another, to collect in full.

For a squabble within our band, it was better not to be armed. I was much smaller than Bull Hump or Walks Like Ox. Smaller, too, than Stone and Takes Risks, and the other men in this argument. But they weren't arguing with me. Perhaps I could mediate.

"Tried to kill…" Bull Hump bellowed.

"Beside him…" a boy interrupted.

"Challenge you now…" Takes Risks yelled.

I stepped between them, holding my hands up. "What's this about?"

They all shouted at me at once.

"Quiet!" I said. "Our headman should speak first, then someone may answer. That's how The People solve disputes."

The custom was for them to do this in front of a wise man, a respected elder. I was old enough and had plenty of experience. But I didn't have Stone's respect. Not much of it, anyway. The same could be said for Bull Hump and Takes Risks. Still, they all grew quiet. Stone puffed himself up, turned, and began addressing me.

"We've discovered who shot Bull Hump. Or who shot at me while we hunted the mammoth. Walks Like Ox did it."

"Did not," Walks Like Ox replied.

Thinks like ox, too, I decided, if this was an example of the clever defense he'd use against Stone's accusation. Definitely not one of our brighter sparks above the fire. I raised a hand and stopped him. "Let Stone finish, then respond."

Stone seemed surprised to be expected to continue. He'd stated what happened. As far as he was concerned, that should be enough. I decided some prompting was in order.

"Why do you say that? Did someone see Walks Like Ox shoot that arrow?"

Takes Risks answered. "We found this hidden among his sleeping robes."

He held up another arrow and I examined it. Well made, undecorated, tipped with sharp flint, and fletched with ptarmigan feathers.

"Do you have the one that struck Bull Hump?" I already knew this was a match.

Bull Hump handed it to me. The second arrow was so like the first there could be no doubt they'd been made by the same hand.

"It's not mine," Ox said. "Someone must have put it in my things."

"Enough," I said. "A band member has been murdered. Another has been shot. Now Walks Like Ox stands accused. We must hold a council. The men must gather and hear the claim that Walks Like Ox shot the arrow. Next, they'll listen to him defend himself. Anyone with knowledge of what happened must speak at the council. Then our band will decide what to do."

◇◇◇

Gathering the men wasn't hard. Most had been drawn to the confrontation. The few still butchering the mammoth, or gathering wood and dung for fires to cure meat, quickly formed a circle around the great fire. Not a very great fire just then, since we needed most of the fuel for curing the mammoth. We'd built a central fire out of habit. We hadn't cooked over it. All of us had gorged on the fresh kill.

Stone took his traditional place at the head of the circle. He held the sacred short lance, the one with which I'd killed the mammoth. It was both a functional tool and a symbol of his leadership. Bull Hump and Takes Risks sat on either side of Stone. Walks Like Ox and his two friends sat across the fire, but within the circle. Crooked Nose and Seven Fingers were both younger than Ox, and much smaller. Crooked Nose had been dropped on his face as a baby. Soon after he learned to walk, Seven Fingers had tried to take meat away from one of the dogs.

No women joined the circle. They had no place there. But they gathered just outside it, listening. Though women may not participate in a band's council, I've heard more than one make pointed comments to her sisters, comments later brought up among the men and acted upon. Women speak among themselves from just beyond our circle, stating how foolish the men must be to make such decisions. Foolish men might sleep alone or expect to prepare their own meals and mend their own clothing. Few men were foolish enough to ignore comments like that, even if they pretended not to hear.

All our men formed the circle. I was inside it. Since I'd called the meeting, leading it was my responsibility. None of the accusers or the accused could do that. And, though the band wouldn't act unless all the men agreed—and none of the women objected too strongly—the person who ran a meeting like this could make lifelong enemies. I wasn't surprised when no one suggested I step aside.

By the time we started, everyone knew what Stone and Bull Hump and Takes Risks accused Ox of doing. It was tradition, though, for someone to explain. I did, beginning with Tall Pine's death, reminding everyone that these latest accusations might have larger implications. I didn't name Tall Pine, of course, nor Hair on Fire. I spoke of lost friends. Of those we buried.

I asked that the two arrows be passed around the circle. And I asked Stone, as headman, to explain how the second arrow was found.

"We discovered it while we searched the camp," Takes Risks answered for him. "It was hidden in Walks Like Ox's bedding."

That led to general muttering among the band. I waited until they quieted.

"Is there any other evidence against Walks Like Ox?"

None of the men spoke, though I heard Gentle Breeze remind someone that our strangled friend had been very strong. It would take another strong man to overcome him. That was likely, if not necessarily true, and there were others as strong as Ox. I didn't mention any of that. I wasn't there to defend him. Not if doing so helped him get Down as his woman. Ox could speak for himself. Or call on others who might sow doubt. Including me.

"It's not my arrow," Ox said. "I've never seen an arrow like this before. I don't say Takes Risks lies when he says he found it in my bedding. But if that's where he found it, someone who wishes to harm me put it there."

Seven Fingers spoke next. "I've never seen an arrow like this, either. I stood beside Walks Like Ox when we killed the mammoth. We were well down the line from Bull Hump and Stone," he said. "Walks Like Ox would have had to turn away from the beast to aim at them. Walks Like Ox had only a few arrows and I saw him shoot all of them at the mammoth."

Crooked Nose said he and Ox had left their bedding out of the tent for young men without women so it would air before the hunt.

"There were no arrows in Walks Like Ox's robes," Crooked Nose said. "Walks Like Ox fletched all his arrows with the feathers of the goose we killed when we camped by the lake thick with waterfowl. I stood between Walks Like Ox and Bull Hump and would have seen if Walks Like Ox shot an arrow toward Bull Hump or Stone. And, if Walks Like Ox had shot it, the arrow couldn't have gone by Stone's ear and would have hit Bull Hump on the other side of his neck."

"The young man makes a good point," I said.

"I stuck my arrows in the ground beside me," Bull Hump said. "One of them fell over. I'd just bent and turned to pick it up when Walks Like Ox shot me. That explains where it struck."

I'd known Bull Hump would have an explanation.

"And I stepped around Bull Hump to get a better shot when the arrow just missed me," Stone said.

Takes Risks pointed at each of the boys. "I think these three planned to replace us as leaders of this band. I think they started with the one who was strangled. If the arrow had flown true, only two of us would be left."

The circle muttered again as the opposing trios glared at each other.

I looked at Crooked Nose. "Have you ever seen this arrow before?"

He shook his head.

"Is there anything else?" I asked the circle.

"It's not my arrow," Ox repeated.

"No," I said. "Walks Like Ox is right. The arrow belonged to the one killed by the mammoth. When I buried him with the things he'll need in the spirit world, I noticed his arrows. They're like the ones we've seen here—undecorated, well made, and fletched with ptarmigan feathers."

The band went so quiet you could hear the mosquitoes hum. Every face turned to me.

"The man we buried couldn't have shot Bull Hump. He left his bow and arrows behind when he took the short spear. But he made his arrows in the company of the other young men without women. He made them with Walks Like Ox and Seven Fingers and Crooked Nose. And slept beside them, where Walks Like Ox and his friends could have stolen some so the one we buried might be blamed for what they did."

"Are you sure, Raven?" It was one of the old men, Claw, named for a deformed hand. I remembered how the council debated whether to raise him or leave him for the wolves when he was born and I was a boy.

I reached inside my robe and pulled out another arrow. "I took this from the one we lost to the mammoth before I covered him with rocks. I knew then whose arrow struck Bull Hump. These three knew whose arrow struck Bull Hump, too. If they didn't shoot it, why not tell us who made it?"

"I challenge them," Bull Hump shouted. "I'll kill all three with my bare hands."

"No," I said. "Which of them deserves to die? Surely not all three. Only one arrow was shot. We don't know who shot it. Only that these three are guilty of lying to us, perhaps to save a friend. Or it's possible the arrow found in Walks Like Ox's bedding was planted by someone else. That person could be the guilty party."

"But that's not likely." Takes Risks nicely summarized the case I'd built against the three.

The boys glared at him.

"Then what?" Stone said.

"Banish them," I said. "Send word to nearby bands so they'll have to find somewhere far away from us to live."

The band grumbled, but they all seemed to agree. All but Bull Hump, who still wanted blood vengeance.

"Later," I said, "if we discover someone else was guilty, we can invite these three to return."

That convinced the women. Bull Hump argued a bit more, but I'd won because I had the women's approval. No innocent would die. The punishment wasn't extreme. When Stone agreed, we were done.

I caught Down's eye. She nodded. I'd found a way to save her from Ox and she knew it.

Interlude

I persuaded Stone to let Ox and his friends take robes packed full of generous shares of meat from the mammoth kill—all each of them could carry. That way, if they found a band to take them in, they wouldn't come empty-handed. Or they could travel far, far away from us before having to feed themselves.

Ox was too angry to speak to me. But Seven Fingers and Crooked Nose had turned more frightened than angry. They suddenly seemed like little boys again. They were being forced out into a world away from most of the people they'd always known. They might not find a band to welcome them. They might have to make their own way. Try to build their own band by stealing women, then running far enough to be sure they wouldn't encounter us again, or the fathers and husbands of the women they stole. Three men, barely old enough to have developed the skills life in this harsh land required. They might not survive.

"Why did you do this to us?" Seven Fingers asked me.

"I saved your lives, at least for now," I told him, feeling more than a little guilty. I'd done it because Ox wasn't the kind of man who would tolerate his woman knowing more than he did. If Stone gave Down to that great dull brute, our band wouldn't develop a skilled healer or an accomplished Spirit Woman.

"You save us by driving us away?" Crooked Nose said.

"Bull Hump is sure Walks Like Ox tried to kill him," I said. "Or maybe all three of you, together. And Stone and Takes Risks believe you and the one we just buried may have conspired to

replace them. If you stayed, you'd have to accept challenges
to fight those three to the death. Would that give you a better
chance?"

"But we didn't do anything."

"You didn't tell us you knew whose arrows they were," I said.
At least that was true. And someone had murdered the man who
was strangled. They might have done that.

"It's a terrible thing that one of our own killed a member of
the band. And now this assault on Bull Hump. The band might
not survive if you stayed and accepted challenges. And it won't
let you stay without accepting them. Stay and our band could
shatter into factions. You three are young and strong. If you're
careful, you should live a long time. Maybe you'll be able to
come back to us some day."

Ox snarled, and Crooked Nose simply turned away. But
Seven Fingers seemed to consider what I'd said. "Help my mother
remember me. And ask the spirits to protect us."

"I already asked them," I said. I didn't mention his mother
because she'd been among those who spoke in favor of banish-
ment.

"Damn the spirits," Ox said, but the other two shushed him,
shouldered their packs, and headed downstream. The wolves
feeding on the mammoth's remains parted around them. I
watched until the pack went back to their feast and the three
disappeared in the forest of willows.

◇◇◇

I climbed above the ledge where the mammoth's carcass lay that
afternoon, searching for evidence to prove I might have actually
seen someone up there, just before Hair on Fire died and Bull
Hump took an arrow. The wolves had come and gone across
the grass, leaving me plenty of tracks, but none of them human.
I don't think I'd have noticed the place where someone had
crouched behind a bush except some of its berries were ripening
and I had a weakness for sweets. Even then, I didn't notice the
crushed vegetation until another of Fire's arrows caught my eye.

So, the arrow that struck Bull Hump had been shot from here. When I looked down at the spot where we'd killed the mammoth, I felt sure this was the place I'd caught a glimpse of someone. From here, the arrow that struck Bull Hump would have passed near Stone—near enough that it might have been aimed at him. I searched for signs of who'd been here and found nothing. One thing was clear. None of the boys I'd helped banish from the band could have shot it. All three had been in the line beside us.

We never visit the graves of our dead, but that's what I did next. I was taught that spirits of the dead hold a deep resentment for the living. They envy us, and want company on their journey to the sky camps where they must wait to be born to The People again. The spirit of a dead person, especially one like Hair on Fire, so recently and savagely slain, was supposed to be especially dangerous. But I didn't believe it.

I wasn't surprised at finding the rocks Down and I stacked over him strewn down the slope. Wolves and a bear had been at him. I'd thought our witch might have come to gather corpse poison. Or cannibalize him. Or to steal Down's pubic hair. Maybe someone had done all those things, but the body had been torn to pieces by animals. An arm was missing, gnawed off, but not by a human. What remained of Fire lay down-slope of the rock shelter.

The tools I'd buried with him were scattered but still near the grave. I couldn't find any trace of Down's hair. It could easily have blown away as soon as the grave was opened. Or been devoured by whatever chewed away his groin.

The only footprints I found were large and clawed. The grizzly and wolves. No human prints, except the ones I left while I was there.

I dragged him and his tools back up to the hole in the rock. After I purified what was left of Hair on Fire again, I replaced the rocks. Then I went back down to the river and washed and purified myself.

As I sat on a rock above the stream, in a spot where the breeze kept most of the mosquitoes from me while I dried, I considered what I'd found and what it meant. I'd managed to persuade myself that Ox and his friends had probably killed Tall Pine. Or that they'd plotted to take over our band, led by Fire, who also could have killed Tall Pine. That's how I'd excused myself for planting the arrow in Ox's bedding. That was how the spirits would have acted if they wanted us to right a wrong. They'd let the mammoth slay Fire and encourage me to persuade the band to rid ourselves of the other three, eliminating our murderers. Now, I had to face facts. The spirits hadn't interfered in our lives. Not to help us, anyway. The person who shot Bull Hump had done so while Ox and his friends and Fire were all down near the mammoth. That meant Tall Pine's murderer was probably still in our midst.

I waved away a few mosquitoes and tried to find a spot where the wind would rid me of the rest. All our men had been down by the mammoth. I was sure of it. That left only women and children. And one particular woman came to mind—brave and clever enough to have done both acts. She'd have had easy access to Fire's arrows since she was coupling with him. I didn't like the idea, but Down had benefited the most from recent events. Tall Pine was dead. She wouldn't be his woman and he wouldn't bother her anymore. If Fire had killed the mammoth and she'd killed or wounded her father or Bull Hump, Fire might have been able to take over leadership of the band almost immediately. If he took Down for his woman it would lend a sense of continuity to the transition. Stone might have even gone along with the idea as a way of retaining at least some power. But I had a hard time imagining Down acting so coldly. I could see her killing Tall Pine in self-defense, but she'd have told us. The band knew Tall Pine. Other women would have spoken up. It wouldn't have been murder. Everyone would know it was self-defense.

I could think of several other candidates for Tall Pine's murderer. But the only good ones were men. Could Down have shot the arrow and someone else have killed Tall Pine? Sure. Why not?

On top of that, we had a witch in our midst. The witch seemed connected to Tall Pine's murder, if Down hadn't done it.

Even if Down had killed once and tried to kill again, I couldn't believe she was the witch. She was too young to have learned the evil craft. Unless we had two witches and the other had been teaching Down for years.

Gentle Breeze had been teaching Down to heal. She was wise enough to master witchcraft and Down to learn it, but witches seldom doubled as healers. Witches lived to hurt, not to heal. And I knew Gentle Breeze and Down too well to believe it of them. I couldn't imagine anyone else in the band who was intelligent enough to master the dark art. My only candidates for killer and weaver of magics would have had to deceive me every day I'd spent in the band with them. If they were that skilled, I doubted I could outwit and catch them anyway.

Dry at last, I shook my head in frustration as I shrugged back into my leathers. Stone and his friends probably thought I'd just caught the murderer, and they knew nothing about the witch. For the moment, they should be satisfied with me. But I was going to be in real trouble with them if the murderer struck again or if the witch left another doll. Unless I got lucky and the witch and murderer made me the next victim.

Flesh

Twelve days later, we'd managed only six days of normal travel. I felt frustrated enough to scream. In fact, I had screamed a few times. Not that it did any good.

All the meat we carried burdened us. There were five fewer men—two dead, three banished—to carry it. Stone and Takes Risks were watching their backs instead of hurrying the band. And Bull Hump's neck still hurt so much that he couldn't be bothered carrying his share.

We camped on another stone outcrop that night. It was colder there. No matter how slow, we'd come much closer to the ice. Closer, too, to the pass I believed led between the mountains and through the glaciers. There were signs that other bands had recently camped on the spot. The smell of smoke on the wind told us more were nearby. Our band had lost five, but we'd added the young couple whose child I'd tried to save. Not the child. The child had died. But the man and his woman joined us willingly enough. Their own band was too far ahead. Alone, they might catch up. But they could just as easily encounter predators or unfriendly strangers. They were safer with us and they knew it. Just as we were safer adding them.

As the tents were pitched and the women began preparing dinner, I noticed an extra tent being raised down-slope on our back trail. A Women's tent. I found Gentle Breeze and asked.

"Down," she said. "The child becomes a woman."

"Good. You told her what to do? The things she must avoid?"

"I told her, though she's known all this for some time."

I understood why Down knew, but gave no sign of it. "Is anyone with her?" The women often shared their cycles. The Earth Mother linked them to trickster moon, who usually eased their burden by not requiring them to face it alone.

"No. Down is a handful of days earlier than most of the women will be. Perhaps you, because you aren't so concerned about such things, can keep an eye on the Women's tent. We don't know this country. I don't like thinking about a young girl alone out there. Walks Like Ox wanted her. He and the other boys may have followed us. Or some other band may need women to bear them children."

"I'll keep an eye on her," I promised.

"But only an eye, Raven," Gentle Breeze warned me. "You're too old for her, and while Stone might give her to you now, he'll regret it later. You'd be in his way. And in Stone's way is not a place you want to be, old man."

I smiled. "Are you jealous, old woman?"

She spat at my feet, but I looked back and caught her smile as I walked away.

◇◇◇

I'd known for years that Down was special, very smart and brave. Maybe too brave for her own good, as in her relationship with Hair on Fire. Once she'd gone exploring in the willows near one of our countless new camps. She'd come upon a dire wolf, surprised him at his kill. Knowing she couldn't outrun him, she'd screamed and thrown stones and even charged him. He must have eaten well, already. Or The Earth Mother favored Down and whispered in the big wolf's ear. The dire wolf growled at the girl, turned, and trotted off into the willows, abandoning his kill to a child then entering her twelfth summer.

Now she interested me because I'd been without a woman for far too long. Except for occasional lessons in technique. Or gifts from old friends, over very quickly so our absence from camp might not be noticed. Lately, especially since I'd learned about Fire and watched her with his corpse, I'd imagined how it might feel to lie with the Down who had become a woman. Until Gentle Breeze told me so, it hadn't occurred to me that it might actually be possible. That I, for the moment at least, might be a logical mate for Stone's daughter. The girl who might be Tall Pine's killer? Who may have shot Bull Hump? Maybe even a would-be witch?

Once the idea that Stone might let me have his daughter was in my head, I couldn't get it out, but I hesitated to raise the possibility with Stone. If he said no, it would be all but impossible to persuade him to change his mind. And I wasn't sure how Down would feel about it. I wanted her, but not at the cost of her resentment. Fire still held a special place in her heart. He might stay there for a long time. But I also dared to dream she might see the advantages of becoming my woman. And I hoped the idea of lying with someone as old and scarred as me wouldn't repel her. Or, worse, make her laugh at such an absurd notion.

I went to Stone that evening. I told him the pass through the mountains and ice needed scouting. Because the course narrowed just ahead of us and we could smell the smoke of other bands, we'd soon find ourselves adjacent to them. We could see their smoke rising—too near in some cases. Too near for people we knew nothing about. I'd take the next few days to look them over. Make contact if it seemed wise. Perhaps we could trade mammoth meat for other foods and necessities, or make alliances to form one great band for the journey through the pass.

Stone agreed. He always felt relieved when I was away from camp. I wasn't a challenge to him physically, but my relationship with the spirits frightened him. He didn't know how to manage someone who might be able to call on the help of invisible friends.

"Keep moving," I told him. "If there's danger ahead, I'll come back to warn you."

Stone agreed, still I decided to return every day to make sure he wasn't using my scout as an excuse to sit and rest.

As soon as we finished the evening meal, I wrapped some mammoth steaks in willow leaves, rolled them with supplies inside my robe, tied it with a spare bowstring, and hung that with my bow and quiver over my shoulders. I carried my spear in my right hand. Stone wasn't paying attention, so I took Snow along this time. We'd be less likely to stumble into predators, human or otherwise. The dog and I jogged down an animal trail toward the stream below our camp. People paused to wave or wish me luck before we disappeared among the willows.

We followed the stream until just below and downwind of the nearest source of smoke. I climbed a rocky ridge to look down on their tents. Snow knew his job, staying silently at my side.

The camp was very small. Only a few tents, more worn than ours. Half-a-dozen adults, though some might have already retired. They looked gaunt and hungry. This group offered no threat. After our recent losses, Stone might offer them the chance to join a richer band such as ours. Their additional numbers might be worth the cost of sharing our current riches. But I'd warn him, too, because I smelled sickness. I'd approached them from downwind so their dogs wouldn't smell us. But I saw no dogs. Had they eaten them out of desperation?

After Snow and I scouted a handful of other bands, none remarkable or obviously dangerous, we used the ridge to make good time back toward our camp. We waded through sedges and swarms of mosquitoes to pass it downwind, so our own dogs wouldn't smell Snow and me. They weren't likely to make a great fuss about us. But I didn't want anyone to know my destination that night.

Twilight, actually. The sun had begun slipping below the horizon the last few nights. That's where it hid as I approached our Women's tent—Down's tent.

The Women's tent is forbidden to men. Dangerous, so most believe. That part didn't trouble me. But how should I approach the girl? And how would she react to me? If I frightened her—if she screamed—they'd hear her in camp. I could probably get away, but I'd be recognized. The best plan was to creep into the tent as quietly as possible, put a hand over her mouth and calm her, tell her who I was, that I meant her no harm. I only wanted to talk.

I told Snow to wait. I slipped everything off my shoulders and lay my spear across my pack. I pulled my knife and dug up one of the willow pegs that fastened the tent's edge to the ground, leaving me room to crawl inside. I'd dropped onto my belly when Down spoke to me.

"Is it your time to bleed, too, Raven?"

I must have jumped, because she giggled. She sat on the ground behind me, ten paces up the side of the ridge. In the dusk, her leathers, tanned skin, and dark hair blended into the browns and grays of the rock face.

"Or have you come, so well armed, to force yourself on me? That you'd violate someone who's bleeding doesn't surprise me. The women talk among themselves, sometimes even in the presence of children. But that you'd feel you needed your dog and all your weapons…"

She mocked me, teasing without cruelty. Still, her humor sounded forced. She radiated melancholy. I wasn't the man she'd hoped to tease this way. She missed Hair on Fire.

I released Snow and he bounded up the slope and caressed her face with his tongue. I envied him.

"Why are you awake, Down? These days will be hard for you. Many women suffer pains through their bleeding, and the burden of carrying your own tent will make it hard for you to keep up with the band as they move.

"I had a dream that something dangerous stalked me. It seems I was right."

I sighed. "I'm no danger to you, Down. No more than you're already in."

Her eyes widened. "What do you mean?"

"You think I don't know who shot Bull Hump?

She didn't deny it.

"And," I continued, "who killed Tall Pine. My duty is to tell the band. To warn them there's a witch in our midst, yet here I am."

"What do you want from me, Raven?"

"I want to save you from yourself, Down. I want to help you, but first I want you to tell me why you killed and tried to kill. Make me understand why you've done these things."

"Maybe you're right," Down said. "Maybe I am in trouble if you think I did them. I thought you were my friend."

"I want to be."

"Well, if it helps, I didn't do either."

I raised an eyebrow. "Then who did?"

"I thought you already knew. I thought that was why you sent the boys into exile. Or I hoped it was at least part of the reason."

"I sent them so you'd be safe from Walks Like Ox."

She nodded. "I know that. And I thank you, but I thought, maybe…"

"Sure," I said. "There's always maybe. But they didn't have anything to do with shooting Bull Hump."

"And neither did I. I was behind the men at the other end of the line from you, hurling rocks, trying to keep the mammoth's attention. Maybe somebody saw me there."

I hadn't. And I'd asked a few people if they knew where Down had been when we killed the mammoth. None did.

"And," Down continued, "I certainly didn't think I needed to do anything that desperate. Right then, I thought Fire was about to become the most popular man in the band. That my father would reward Fire with me. That the gift would keep Fire under my father's control and strengthen his leadership of the band. All I'd have to do was announce my first bleeding, and then…"

A tear slid down her cheek. "That ought to prove I'm not your witch. The man I wanted is dead. Now who will I end up with? Bull Hump or Takes Risks? Maybe I should just walk off into the tundra and let the wolves have me."

"Would you consider becoming my woman?" I asked. "If you can't stand the thought of lying with me, we could fake that part. Lie under the robes and thrash around and grunt a little, to convince the others. The rest of the time you'd continue study-ing healing under Gentle Breeze and me. And you'd become my pupil. I'd teach you to be a Spirit Woman. I know how clever you are and I'm impressed by the wisdom you already possess. I want to help you live the life you deserve, to survive and be happy."

"Oh, Raven. You're very kind, but how can I ever be happy without Fire?" Her tears came faster and she began to sob.

I have a weakness for crying women. I feel their pain and blame myself for not making things better. Illogically, I believe curing their hurt is up to me. I had no way to fix Down's hurt. No way to bring Fire back.

"You really shouldn't keep mentioning his name. It's one thing for me to do it. Another for one he'd loved to speak it and call to his spirit."

"I wish I *could* call his spirit to me."

I reached out my hand to wipe a tear from her cheek. She looked up at me with such terrible sadness. I took her in my arms and she came willingly enough. Her body shook. I held her and rocked her and stroked her hair. Finally, she whispered something into my chest. I couldn't understand. I found her chin and raised it so I could hear her.

"I miss him so, Raven. You hear the spirits. You communicate with them. Can't you bring him back?"

I bent and kissed the tears from her cheeks. Some of them had run onto her lips and I kissed those, too. I couldn't give her Hair on Fire, but I could give her his need for her. Her lips opened under mine. My hands found the laces of her leathers, loosened them. I touched her small breasts. The place between her legs. I gave her Fire's desire and my knowledge of the things that pleased women. She cried out, softly, and then I found ways to make her cry out again. Over and over until it was she who demanded more. She who rode me until we were both beyond exhaustion.

"You are Fire," she whispered as she lay atop me, grinding her pelvis against my own.

I wasn't. Her need for him combined with her inability to understand how someone else could make her feel these things. I did feel Fire's need to touch her through me. I should have explained to her that this was as close as he'd ever come to her again. But I wanted to join her this way many, many more times. I wanted Down to desire me as much as I desired her. So I said nothing to deny it. I pressed myself against her and touched the places I knew would make her forget everything but the pleasures of the flesh. I delayed my own gratification until I felt the pulse of her complete surrender. And then matched it with my own.

Ivory

Bone

I should have been too exhausted to dream, and yet I was back in that strange place where cold fire burned along the roof and every corner was exactly square. The perfect woman and the man with ice eyes were at it again. Though his mask lay elsewhere. Both of them were naked. She, teasing him, arousing him, refusing to satisfy. He, enjoying it but increasingly frustrated and demanding.

This time the perfect woman no longer seemed so perfect. I recognized something false about her. She wasn't doing this for pleasure. She had another purpose which troubled me. Or would have troubled me if I'd been her partner. I saw her in a new light—in comparison with Down. This one might have larger breasts, and fuller hips. More dramatic curves. But Down had something else. Something fresh and real.

My skull lay on the flat wooden surface again. Near the edge, as if I were a necessary prop for this couple's mating rituals. And she was easy enough to watch, or had been. Now, my eyes wandered around this strange hut. There were things I recognized beside me on that flat slab of wood. Stone tools—flint scrapers and a spear point. An obsidian blade—sharp and brittle. Carved mammoth ivory. At the far corner of my eye lay something hauntingly familiar, just beyond my ability to see it. Strange, I decided, since even without eyes I could only look ahead of myself, as I had when I was flesh and not just bone.

With that thought, suddenly I could see all around me, including the thing I'd been trying to make out. Ivory—a carving. An Earth Mother figurine. I recognized it because I'd made it years before—a gift for my woman. The one who'd been washed away as we crossed that icy river. I'd made the figure while I courted her. Before I won her. Before I lost her.

Her name was Willow. I'd used her face and slim, supple figure in my effort to portray The Earth Mother. As a result, this image of The Goddess was longer and leaner than the few others I'd seen, a vision of Willow with the bulge of pregnancy I'd hoped to give her. She'd worn that carving on a leather thong around her neck every day. She'd been wearing it when the waters took her. How could this pair have it?

Willow's statue had yellowed and worn smooth with age. Great age, if Ice Eyes had told the truth about how long my skull lay in the earth before he found me.

"Where did you get this?" I demanded in my mind, having no tongue or lips or breath with which to shape the words.

"What?" he said. "Who?"

The girl did something to refocus his attention. But I sensed he'd heard me. Could I communicate with him? What should I ask? And what was that noise I'd just heard?

"Now. I want you now," the girl told him, suddenly eager for what she'd been avoiding. He took her as the entry to the hut opened and another perfect woman appeared.

The man saw the second woman just as she saw him.

"No," I heard the man call out.

The new woman echoed him in his mind, and in mine. "No."

The second woman looked more mature than the perfect one, whose arms and legs enwrapped the man's body. I had a strange feeling the second woman wasn't much younger than I. Or than I'd been when I went to sleep. Yet she showed no signs of age. Her hair was rich and full and dark. Her face remained as free of lines as Down's. But her shape was fuller and there was something about her eyes. A hardness. And shock just now, but not surprise. Weariness, I thought, at repeated disappointments.

She spoke the man's name, though it made no sense to me. I heard it through his mind, and even there, it seemed only sounds without meaning. I was Raven, the black bird filled with wisdom and given to tricks. Down was the soft feathers you found on waterfowl. Ice Eyes real name was only random noises.

"You promised me this would never happen again," the second woman said.

"Again?" the perfect woman said, unconcerned by her nakedness. She hadn't stopped grinding against the man, even though he'd wilted and fallen out of her. At the moment, he was more interested in covering himself than in continuing to mate with the perfect woman.

"Who's this little violator of my rights as your woman?" the new woman asked. That isn't the right translation, but it's the sense of the uncomplimentary term she used.

The second woman wore fine skins, though they were duller in color than what the perfect one had worn. And she wore more layers of them. Bright hoops dangled from her ears and a ring adorned with a fabulous crystal decorated one slender finger.

"This isn't what it looks like," Ice Eyes told her. If I hadn't been only a skull, I would have laughed out loud. What else could it be?

The man glanced around in panic, a strange look on his face. "Who laughed?"

"Me, you fool," I thought.

"Who said that?" the man demanded.

He *had* heard me.

"Oh, I see," the second woman said. "You're going to pretend you're having mental problems. That this is part of some confused episode. Are you about to tell me that until this moment you didn't realize what the two of you were doing? The insanity defense? Nice try." She turned and stormed back toward the entrance to the shelter.

"Yeah," the perfect one said. "Cut the crap. Tell her about us. Tell her you're leaving her for me."

"Maybe she'd believe a fertility ceremony," I thought. "Something to increase your band's numbers."

"Fertility ceremony...?"

He heard me the same way I'd been hearing him.

"Oh, brother," the second woman said. She left the hut, slamming a piece of wood that neatly fit the exit as she left.

"You'll have to admit our relationship to her now," the perfect one said. "Leave her. Do it, and you can have me anytime you want. I'll see that you're put in charge of our dig program. You can open any site, anywhere. Don't leave her, and you'll never dig again. Never touch me again, either."

"Who cares?" I thought at him. "Tell me where I am and why I'm just a skull."

His eyes got very large as they turned to me.

"Skull," he whispered. He grabbed his leggings, pulled them on, and went through the shelter's exit like a fox bolting from camp after sneaking in and grabbing someone's lunch.

The perfect one stood, hands on those magnificent hips.

"You arranged this," I thought at her. "You planned this to trap him."

The perfect woman showed no indication of hearing me. Apparently, only the man could do that. And I, him.

The perfect woman slipped into her skins. She reached inside a brightly colored pack and took out something she held in front of her face while she smoothed the brilliant red paint she used to color her lips and added more. She painted her eyes and cheeks with other tools. As she put them back in her pack, she glanced at the flat place where I sat.

Her mouth opened as she asked a question I'd understand soon enough.

◇◇◇

"What's this?"

For a moment I was certain the perfect woman said it.

My eyes flew open. I was confused, wondering where the perfect woman had gone. Wondering what Blue Flower was doing in my dream. Wondering how I could be so lucky as to lie beneath a robe snuggled against Down's unclothed body.

"Raven!" Blue Flower screeched. "You evil old man. You're not allowed near a woman during her bleeding. You know that."

My tongue was faster than it should have been. "I follow the instructions of the spirits, Blue Flower, not the superstitions of The People."

Blue Flower bent and snatched the robe away from us, exposing our nakedness. Now, she truly screamed. Loud enough that I knew they'd hear her in camp. Stone and Bull Hump and Takes Risks would come running, armed, thinking Blue Flower had met a bear or a lion or hunters of women from another band.

"You haven't just been with her in this tent," Blue Flower howled in outrage. "You've raped her. You've raped Stone's child."

Down shouldn't have said a thing, but I wasn't surprised when she did.

"Actually, Blue Flower, I raped him."

Blue Flower's jaw dropped. When she spoke again, her voice was little more than a horrified whisper.

"You two have committed crimes against the spirits. You both must be punished. Otherwise, the spirits will damn us. Send sickness and bad luck and our band will perish."

"No, no, no," I said. "Only Down and I are at risk and I can protect us."

I wasn't worried about the spirits, but I had to admit I wasn't sure I could protect Down and myself from her father's wrath. The entire band's, actually. But Blue Flower was no longer there. She'd spun on her heel. The meat and roots and berries she'd brought for Down's breakfast lay scattered at our feet. Blue Flower sprinted along the ridge toward camp. And, from the camp, others ran to meet her.

"Down," I said. "There are times for explaining and times for running. This is a time to run."

She gestured at our bodies. "Naked?"

I judged the distance between camp and the Women's tent. "Put on your moccasins. Bundle everything else you'll need. No provisions. We may be running for some time."

I began looking for my boots. I found one near where I'd left my pack at the edge of the tent. The other, just below where we'd coupled. I grabbed my things and rolled them with Down's into the robe with which she'd covered us. She grabbed a small pack from the tent.

"Time to go," I said. Stone was bellowing my name.

"Lead the way," Down said. "I'll be behind your behind."

I scrambled up the side of the ridge above the Women's tent. Snow bounced around us, delighted at the chance to join in our run. It would be more of a climb for the men from camp to get up here than it was for us. And they wouldn't remember there was a game trail on the other side leading down to a great mass of willows and another wandering stream bed. We'd be down there and out of sight by the time they reached the top. Once among the willows, wading through the frigid stream, we'd make it very hard for them to follow us.

"Where are we going?" Down was breathing easier that I.

"Just follow." I couldn't be more specific because I didn't know.

"Yes, Raven. I'm on your skinny ass." She laughed and proved it by patting each of my cheeks.

I laughed, too, and lengthened my stride to lead us deeper in the willows. Before the day ended, I planned to also pat her buttocks, the beginning moves of a coupling such as the one that exhausted us the night before.

◇◇◇

I expected the band's hunters to run themselves out long before they did, but rage is a powerful emotion. Stone must have had it in abundance, though they never managed to gain on us. Down was young and strong. She had the inexhaustibility of youth. I had stamina. I'd never been one of our fastest. But even though

I'd grown old, I could still run all day. I'd often chased down wounded animals before wolves or other predators got to them. I ducked and danced among the willows, using the streambed occasionally when another stream joined this one or we rounded a rocky spot where we might have taken another path. We'd continue running as long as I could hear them behind us.

The stream widened as we followed it north, well ahead of our band. As it widened, so did the stand of willows. They grew thicker and taller as well. At a rocky spot where our footprints would be hard to see, I ducked off the animal trail we followed and dropped almost to my knees to get through a clump of willows. As I rose, looking for another trail, I realized the clearing we'd entered wasn't empty. I tried to stop. But Down was right behind me. She plunged through the same hole I'd taken, head lowered to save her eyes from the branches. Her head rammed my rump and sent me tumbling until I lay nose to nose with the great bear.

I might have screamed in terror, but suddenly, I had no air in my chest. When Down saw the animal, her voice worked just fine.

"Get away, you ugly thing," she commanded. She threw her bundle at him and then bent, picking up stones. My nose was only a few fingers from the beast's jagged teeth. It could snap its jaws or swing a paw and end my life. It did neither, as surprised to find me in its face as I was to be there.

◇◇◇

Once, long before I froze in panic, facing instant death nose-to-nose with a great bear among the willows, with only Down's shouts and hurled stones to protect me, a legend among The People visited us. It happened in the old country, before we began our migration or I left my father's band. He was named Beast Slayer because he feared no animal and had hunted them all. The man's reputation was so great that a crowd gathered to listen to him. Men asked questions. Boys crawled between brawny legs to hear what he said. I was one of those boys. I didn't hear who asked, but I remember Beast Slayer's reply.

"No. There is one animal I'm afraid of. I won't stalk a great bear alone."

I'd shivered in delighted terror, knowing there was an animal even Beast Slayer dreaded.

"You all know how to kill a great bear. Every man and dog in the band fights him. We lose half the dogs, and some of the men. The dogs keep the bear busy long enough for the men to place their spears and arrows." He touched his body to show where the most damage might be done.

"We stay out of the bear's reach and make him bleed. Hurt him enough and even a great bear dies. That'd be something to celebrate if then we didn't have to bury our own dead."

Our men muttered agreement.

"I've heard there are two ways to kill a great bear single-handed. I can't explain the first because the man who planned to show me was torn to shreds before he could even set up his weapons.

"The second method works. I witnessed it. A great bear killed a man's woman and children. The man went to the sacred mountain and prayed to the spirits for revenge. They took pity on him and gave him a vision of how it could be done. The man cut segments of ribs from the skeleton of a mammoth and bound them together with sinew. He found the longest straight limb he could from a hardwood tree, shaped it, sharpened one end, and hardened the point by firing it. He lashed a flat slab of wood on the other end. Then he carved and shaped a short ivory staff and cut grooves along its length. He shaped obsidian blades and bound them in those groves, sharp edge out. He showed me how the blades would shave the soft hair from his arms. When all these things were ready, he went after the great bear that killed his family.

"He used the ribs as a shield. He planted the base of his spear on the ground and aimed its tip just under the bear's ribs. He provoked the animal to charge him and impale itself on the spear. The flat piece of wood at the spear's base kept it from being driven into the ground or from sliding. The bear had to push the spear completely through its body to reach the man. The man lay, hidden beneath his shield, using one arm to reach out and slash the bear with the obsidian-edged staff, cutting the animal again and again. He slashed at the bear's mouth and throat and cut open its tongue. It took a long time, but the bear died on top of his shield. In spite of the ribs, the man was badly injured. Still, he managed to crawl from under the beast and take its head. He brought the head back to me. I'd watched the fight from nearby. And I watched, when he died of his wounds."

Every word Beast Slayer said all those years ago flashed through my mind as I kneeled among the willows and looked death in his toothy face. For a long moment, nothing happened. Then, instead of biting or clawing me, the bear laughed. It was a deep, rumbling laugh, but not so deep as I might have expected from such a broad chest. A paw flashed up to knock away one of Down's stones and failed. She had a strong arm and a good aim and the stone hit the bear in the shoulder.

"Ouch!" the bear said. A thick human arm swept up from inside the bear's chest and threw its head aside. A man's head appeared where the bear's had been.

"You're not a bear," I said, quick to note the obvious. Maybe I can be excused since I expected to die a very ugly death at any moment. Even then, I wasn't sure whether this was a man wearing the skin of a great bear or a great bear who'd decided to appear to us as a man.

"I'm not a bear," the bear said, "and I won't hurt you. So please make the girl stop throwing stones."

I looked over my shoulder. Down, glorious in her literally naked rage, stood poised with another rock. She didn't put it down but she didn't hurl it, either.

"I won't throw more rocks," she said, "if you promise not to harm Raven."

"Good," the bear said. "Now, you two wait for me here. I'll go scare off those people chasing you. Then I'll come back and explain why I'm wearing this bear skin and you can tell me why you're wearing nothing but your bare skins."

He laughed at his joke, put the bear head back in place, and waded into the willows.

"Should we wait or keep running?" Down asked.

My heart raced. My arms and legs had gone numb and tingly. Dry-mouthed, I felt too weak to move and nearly too weak to answer.

"Stay," I whispered.

Down helped me dress, then dressed herself. She dabbed mud on us to keep off the mosquitoes. I didn't feel aroused even when she touched intimate places. Meeting the bear had left me empty, incapable of making decisions. I'd trapped Down with me in my stupor. We did what he'd asked—waited for the man bear to have a second chance to kill us.

Figurine

I must have dozed. I'm not sure how. I should have questioned the man who'd been a bear before he left us. I should have consulted with Down about waiting for this stranger. There'd been something peculiar about him. He was huge. Big enough to wear the bear's skin and make it seem real. And his face…There'd been something different about that, too. The shape wasn't quite what I was accustomed to on members of The People.

I'd noticed these things, but I couldn't concentrate on them. Down had doubts about waiting. I should have led her to a safe spot to watch the man bear when he returned and then decide what to do about him.

I heard the shouts of the men pursuing us turn to panic-stricken cries. The man bear must have showed himself. After that, their voices receded rapidly as they ran for their lives. That should have pleased me. But I'd entered some trance-like state. Something like what I'd tried to do when I sought the vision that gave me my secret name and directed the way I lived my life.

I'd survived in these willows when I expected to die. The man bear might not have harmed me, but the experience numbed my soul. Or separated it from my body so I couldn't think properly.

I slipped into a waking dream, though I remained aware of Down and the frightened voices of our band in the distance.

Bone

While Down and I ran from Stone, met the bear, then waited for his return, the sun had made half a circle across a bright blue sky swept clean of clouds. But in my dream, Perfect Woman stood exactly where she'd been when Blue Flower woke us.

The perfect one turned toward the flat place my skull always occupied. This time, she looked at something next to me.

She stepped to the edge of the surface and picked up the carving I'd made of Willow.

"No," I told her. "You don't deserve to touch it."

That didn't stop her. She turned Willow's likeness in her hand, examining every surface. The way she caressed it with her fingers was erotic.

Though the carving had worn terribly from when I'd last seen Willow wear it, it remained an object of considerable beauty. Perhaps I should have felt pleased that this woman obviously appreciated that. But I didn't.

She rubbed it against her face, closing her eyes to better feel its texture. I wished I'd left a sharp edge on it rather than polishing it so carefully. I also wished Ice Eyes had hidden the thing so Perfect Woman would never have seen it.

I shouted at her. "Put it down. Leave it alone." She couldn't hear me.

Instead, she opened that brightly colored pouch at her waist and placed the figurine inside. She headed for the hut's entry. I'd have stopped her with the spear that should have been attached to that sharpened flint point next to me, if I'd had a body to go with my skull.

As she went through the exit, something crashed to the floor of the hut. Now that I knew how, I looked to see what it was, even though the edge of the flat wooden surface blocked my normal sight. The flint point I'd wanted to hurl at her lay on the strangely patterned and flat surface where I'd assumed a dirt floor must be. The point had shattered. Several shards broke away when it hit that odd, hard floor.

She turned and looked back, as puzzled as I.

How did that happen? She hadn't brushed against it when she took the carving. No other living being was in the hut. Just Perfect Woman and me—a skull. A skull that could talk to Ice Eyes, but not her. A skull, whose vision wasn't limited to what he'd once seen from inside his eye sockets. A skull, that had become angry enough to manipulate a tool it could no longer touch…?

If so, I'd failed. I might have moved the spear point, but I hadn't sent it flying into her flesh. I thought about trying again. The obsidian blade was so much sharper. But before I fully formed the idea, Perfect Woman turned and left, leaving the broken point where it lay.

My mind might have thrown the point at her, but far too weakly. Her departure gave me no second chance. And ended my brief reunion with the image of a woman who'd drowned so long ago. Enraged by Perfect Woman's greed, I tried to hurl a chert scraper toward the place she'd gone. The scraper only tumbled over on its side. It didn't even reach the wooden slab's edge. Clearly, moving things in this world was a skill I had yet to master.

◇◇◇

I changed worlds again to face our bear lumbering back into the clearing. He walked like a bear, though he carried the bear skin in a great roll strapped to his back instead of wearing it over his head and shoulders. Now that I knew, I understood that the great bear who'd greeted us in this clearing had been too narrow through the shoulders. And, of course, lacked every part of a bear's hindquarters. Behind chest, head, and paws, only skin and fur had dragged along the ground.

Our bear laughed again. "Well, now you aren't bare and I'm not bear."

My mind still reeled from things happening so fast, here and in my dream. But I could think again. This man might be dangerous. He was different. Very tall. Very broad. Dressed all in furs, I thought. Then I realized his body was simply matted with more hair than anyone I'd ever known before. He wore only a breechclout and boots. Was his hair thick enough to protect him from mosquitoes? Since he ignored them, other than to swipe at the ones hovering near his face, it must be. How convenient.

Dark, intelligent eyes peered from beneath a heavy brow. Yellow teeth smiled from a broad jaw with a prominent chin. Then I saw it. A single ornament hung from his neck on a leather strap—the same ornament the perfect woman in my dreams had stolen moments before…and yet in some unthinkably distant future. I'd carved it for Willow who died nearly twenty summers ago. What was going on? What was happening to me?

"Where'd you get that?" I pointed at his chest and realizing I'd just—fifteen thousand years from now—asked the same thing of Ice Eyes.

The stranger lifted it gently in his large hand and showed it to me. "This? My father found it at the edge of a river he crossed before I was born."

Dawn had been looking carefully at him. "Are you a member of The People?"

Our bear grinned with his big yellow teeth. "Yes, or so my mother tells me." He seemed a good-humored, patient sort.

My attention was still fixed on the carving. "I made that. And lost it along with something even more valuable when we crossed a river. Did your father find anything else?"

"Why don't you ask him?"

He spoke clearly, but his voice rang deep and thick, almost as if a bear said the words. He might be a member of The People, but I didn't think all of his ancestors had been.

"When may I speak to your father?"

Our bear shrugged his shoulders, massive for a man if not for a great bear. He looked at the ivory woman in his hand and then back at me. "Why not come and meet him now? If the two of you follow me, I'll take you to my band's camp and feed you well. You can meet him then. We can begin understanding each other better."

Down seemed fine with the idea. "It's not like we have any-place else to go."

"And, if you come," he said, "I'll give you back this carving, as long as Mother agrees."

Snow came barreling through the willows at that moment. Wagging his tail and jumping up to put his feet on my shoulders, then Down's. While he licked our faces, the stranger reached out and scratched Snow's ears. Snow wagged his tail even harder and gave the man nearly as enthusiastic a greeting as he'd given Down and me.

I'd never seen Snow accept a stranger like that before. My doubts softened. Snow didn't think he was a danger. Neither would I.

The Bear of the Cave Clan

We walked toward where the sun dipped lowest. Back in the general direction of the mammoth we'd killed and the place we'd camped when Tall Pine was murdered. We followed game trails that wound through the willows beside the stream.

"How did you get the skin?" I asked the big man.

"With some obsidian knives and good scrapers."

Was he teasing?

"No." I understood that skinning the pelt off a great bear would require good blades and much patience. "How did you kill him?"

"Well," he said, "I didn't want to cut the skin, so I used my club."

My jaw dropped. I wished Beast Slayer had lived long enough to hear this.

"You clubbed a great bear to death? How many of you did it take and how many died?"

"Oh, it wasn't like that." The man showed me his teeth again. "Just me and Mother. The bear had grown fat and slow. He was getting ready to hibernate. Mother explained to him that we needed his skin. So he hardly tried to kill me at all. I had to concentrate on breaking his neck without damaging his pelt. Or letting him claw or bite me. He fought a little because of his pride. But he was much easier to kill than I expected. Because of Mother, I think."

"Your mother must be very persuasive," I said.

"What were you doing with the bear skin today?" Down wondered. "Are you a Spirit Man like Raven? Did we interrupt some ceremony?"

He shook his head. "I'm no Spirit Man. Mother takes care of things like that for us. She's the greatest Spirit Woman ever. She told me to take the skin and go upstream until I was just north of your camp. She said I should put on the skin and wait for you. So I did."

"Wait for us?" I asked.

"Yes. She said you'd come to me. She knows things before they happen. She said I'd frighten you, but you'd wait for me while I scared off the people chasing you."

He nodded his head enthusiastically. "She's good, isn't she? When she tells us what the future will bring, she never gets it wrong."

"I may be a man of the spirits," I said, "though I'm hardly as skilled as your mother." I considered telling him that I'd dreamed while we waited for him and that my dreams were very hard to understand. Except for the possibility that my skull might one day lie in front of a perfect woman and a man with eyes of ice. Thinking that suddenly made it seem too real. I stayed silent.

"She said you were a Spirit Man. She told me that's why we need you."

I had no idea how to respond to that. Until these strange dreams began, my interactions with the world of spirits had mostly been explaining to others why we should do the things we'd been taught. Things like dealing with our dead or releasing the souls of the animals we harvested so their spirits could leave their bodies and join all the others in the sky. That, and purifying the band and guiding our people to follow The Mother's Way. I'd conducted the rituals and sought visions, but my dreams hadn't been more insightful than anyone else's. Our band needed a man of the spirits, so I became one. Less because the spirits spoke to me than because I needed a purpose to survive. Especially after Stone took over the band's leadership with the help of his friends.

"And me?" Down said. "Did your mother mention me as well?"

"Oh, yes," he said. "She told me Raven would be in the company of a beautiful young woman. And she was right. She said I had to persuade you to visit us, too."

"Right." Down grinned. "I must be at least as important to her as Raven."

"No," the big man shrugged. "She said you're more important."

He showed his teeth again and Down smiled with him. She thought he teased her. I thought he meant it, and wondered what we were getting ourselves into.

◇◇◇

"We're here," Bear Man said. That was his name. He'd told us as we followed a series of creeks and then climbed the base of a mountain our band had passed a day before. Near the bottom, we came to a steep cliff that curled off toward the east, where the sun would rise once we began experiencing normal nights again. I couldn't see any evidence of people or habitation and I wondered if our friend was making some kind of joke. Not that he seemed inclined to them. Then a clump of blueberries at the foot of the cliff swung aside. It had masked a narrow opening into a not much wider canyon. An old man with white hair stepped out of the shadows and gave us a friendly wave.

"Good," the old man said. "You're here, Raven. And you, Down. The Mother will be pleased."

How did he know our names? Then I recognized him. His hair was longer and whiter now, but he was Sings While He Works, one of the elders Stone had persuaded to walk into the snow last winter for the good of the band.

Down ran to him and threw her arms around him. "I've missed your songs."

"Then I'll sing for you later. But first, come see who else is here."

Down stuck her head behind the blueberries and cried out in delight. "One Arm! Walks in Darkness!" She ran into the canyon behind the bush and out of my sight.

One Arm and Walks in Darkness were the children who'd also walked into the snow.

"How is it that you have our people?" I asked Bear Man.

"We've been following your band for a long time. Mother told me where to find them. She said Stone didn't want them anymore, so she sent me to gather them and bring them to her. We have more than a few of your strays."

He led me behind the blueberries. I embraced Sings While He Works, Hungry Woman, and the children, our winter's snow hunters. Then Bear Man introduced me to all manner of people, most of whose names I forgot as soon as I met the next person. Their camp clustered about the opening of a cave where still others lived. They were a large band. Almost double our size. But they consisted of an unusual number of the old and lame.

"How do you feed so many?" I almost asked how they kept so many who couldn't contribute to feeding themselves, but several who qualified for that description were nearby and I didn't want to hurt their feelings. Besides, I'd argued against any of the people from our band exposing themselves to the winter's cruel cold.

"Mother provides," Bear Man said.

An old man ambled out of the cave. He caught my eye immediately because he looked so much like Bear Man. He was shorter, broad-shouldered, and broad-faced with dark eyes that burned beneath heavy brows. His arms and legs were thick with muscle and covered with hair, like Bear Man's.

"This is my father," Bear Man said. "His name is Mammoth Rider, because he did so on a bet when he was young. I believe you have questions for him."

The old man grinned and hugged me hard enough that I thought my ribs might crack. When he spoke, his voice was even deeper than Bear Man's, and laced with an accent that made me think The People's tongue wasn't the first he'd learned. It took me a moment to understand that he'd greeted me by name and said he'd heard much about me. How could he?

I pointed at the figurine hanging from Bear Man's neck. "Your son told me you found this pendant in the water of a distant river. I carved it. When I last saw it, it hung from the neck of a young woman. She was swept away and drowned as we crossed that river."

Willow had been at my side one moment—gone the next. She must have stepped in a hidden hole or lost her footing on a slippery rock. I should have been holding onto her. The water was chest deep with a swift, icy current. It snatched her. I dropped everything I carried and threw myself after her. For a long time, there was no sign she'd ever existed. Then, for the briefest moment, Willow's arms reached into the air, already twenty paces farther downstream than I'd gone. I plunged after her. Tried to follow. Tried to find her. I never saw her break the surface again. And I nearly didn't find the surface, either. Somehow, just as my consciousness ebbed, my numb hands brushed against a floating willow trunk. I grabbed it and pulled my way up till I could gasp for air. When I had my breath again, I managed to guide the trunk back into shallow water and claw my way onto a bank. Our band had been astonished to see me alive again. They'd made camp at the edge of the river above where Willow disappeared and had already begun mourning both of us.

I looked in the old man's eyes. "Did you find the woman's body?"

"He did." Another voice spoke from within the shadows of the cave. "He found my body. And then he cared for it until my soul found a way to return and take possession of it once again."

I turned as Willow stepped out of the cave. Her hair was white as snow, though otherwise she seemed hardly changed at all. The years had treated her gently.

I wasn't sure how to react. I'd loved her so deeply. Missed her so much. Been sure she was dead for so many years. And now I'd come here with Down.

"Mother," Bear Man said.

His voice was echoed throughout the camp. "Mother," they all said. And bowed in respect. Awe, maybe.

"Willow?" I whispered, not quite believing it.

"Willow's here," she said. Her voice was different. Deeper, fuller, more commanding. "But hers wasn't the only spirit to find its way into this body."

I felt a chill as she drew nearer. As if her body had never warmed after emerging from the terrible cold of that river.

"Not the only spirit?" I repeated.

"It's your fault," she said. "You carved an Earth Mother with Willow's features. You made me curious, Raven. Caused me to wonder what it would be like to share her flesh and not just her image."

"Are you saying…?"

"You may call me Willow or you may call me Mother," she said. "Because I am both the woman you knew and The Earth Goddess you worship."

She had been in the river too long. It had affected her mind.

"The river killed Willow" she said. "Mammoth Rider is a skilled shaman, an expert in a form of forgotten magic. He called Willow's spirit back. But Willow was beyond the ability to come alone. She could only live again if I lived with her. It has amused me to do so. For now, it suits my purposes. One of those involves you, Raven."

Had I slipped into yet another impossible dream? If I looked down would I discover I was only skull again?

"There's been a murder in the band from which you and I came. All the spirit world cries out for vengeance. You'll deliver it."

I shook my head in confusion and denial.

Willow whispered this time, but her words rang clearly inside my head. "You must do this, or the perfect woman will possess our world and blunt my power. If that happens, your spirit will never join the others among the campfires in the stars. You won't be reborn over and over. Your future lives will forever end right here, with your soul trapped inside a skull for all eternity."

◇◇◇

The people who formerly belonged to our band had questions about their friends and relatives. It wasn't until after a meal of fresh roast caribou that Down and I were able to talk privately. Even then, the mound of soft grasses covered by skins and robes where we were to sleep lay too close to similar sleeping places for us to feel any privacy.

"Who's The Mother?" Down whispered.

"Her name is Willow," I told her softly. "Or was Willow. She says she's Willow but also The Earth Mother."

"Can she be both?"

I remembered the way Willow's voice changed when The Mother spoke. And how different her personality had become.

I shrugged and shook my head. I really didn't know. If she was Willow, and she certainly appeared to be, her near-death in the river had changed her. I supposed she could be The Earth Mother. I'd spoken to The Earth Mother countless times in my years as Spirit Man. This would be the first time she'd answered. Or someone had. So, while I doubted, I wasn't sure. How could she know about my dream if she were only Willow?

"She's definitely not the Willow I used to know," I told Down.

"Someone said Willow was your woman once."

Did I detect a hint of jealousy? I hoped so.

"Yes, long before you were born. She was a kind and clever girl. Not as clever or brave as you, but you'd have liked her. This woman looks like Willow. Says she's Willow, but then she speaks with a different voice and claims to be The Earth Mother. I don't know what to make of her."

Down snuggled against me under the privacy of our robes. "Did you love her?"

I admitted I had. "I mourned her for a very long time. But she's been dead to me for twenty years. I hope you understand you're the only one I love now."

"Thank you," Down said

"Whatever this Willow is, she's not the woman I loved. This one scares me."

"As much as Bear Man did when we met him in the clearing?" Down teased.

"More," I admitted, "but in a different way."

"Don't worry," Down nuzzled my ear. "I'll protect you from her. Didn't I protect you when we thought Bear Man was real?"

I admitted that, too. "You were very brave, though you should have been smart instead. You should have turned and run. You should have..." I stopped thinking about what she should have done because she began touching me in a way that refocused my mind.

"I'm not sure we should..." I looked around the dimness of the cave to see whether people were watching us. They weren't. And from the movements beneath other robes, many of them had similar things on their minds. Then I saw Willow's pale eyes on the far side of the cave. They stared straight at me and didn't seem to blink. It felt like they looked into my soul. I'd been aroused. Suddenly, I wasn't.

"What's wrong?" Down whispered.

"Willow's watching."

"I don't mind. Maybe we can teach her something."

"Maybe we could find a private spot," I suggested.

Down shook her head. "No. Here in front of her, or not at all."

"I'm sorry," I apologized. "I can't."

Down turned away from me. I knew I'd regret this, but what I'd said was true. I wasn't capable of satisfying Down with Willow looking on. Not this new, strange Willow. I looked across the cave again and saw a small smile beneath The Mother's pale, unblinking eyes.

◇◇◇

I woke hours later. Down had cuddled into me in her sleep and I'd been dreaming of her firm young body. I peeked from under our robes. Willow no longer sat where she had. I didn't look for her elsewhere. Instead, I ducked my head back into the darkness of our robes and gently touched Down. Here, and here. Stroked there. Rubbed against her. She half woke and responded sleepily. Then with enthusiasm. Finally, with a ferocity that consumed both of us. And scared me, in its own way.

◇◇◇

I couldn't sleep. I dreaded another visit to the place where I was skull. Especially after the threat Willow made.

I slipped quietly from the robes that had been loaned us, pulled on my skins, and stuffed my feet in my boots. I grabbed my spear and stole softly from the cave and through the blueberries onto the side of the mountain. I found a flat rock just down slope from the cave and sat on it. The spot was high enough that I could see a very long way. A herd of caribou followed the valley below, headed toward the same gap in the mountains and ice our band and so many others planned to take to the land Grandfather Eagle promised us. Those herds would feed us as we went. Apparently the spirits smiled on our journey, but they didn't seem to be smiling on me.

I'd cured Down's hurt, for now at least. That was something in my favor. I'd planned for us to talk over our future today. Should we head south on our own? Maybe try to find another band that would accept us. Willow's obviously wouldn't. Not after her instructions to me last night. Or should I collect some fine pelts, maybe including that dire wolf's I'd thought might please Stone? After a few days away from our band, we could try going back. Everyone would have cooled down. I'd find a spot above the band, a place from which I could make another hurried exit if Stone was still intent on punishing us. If Stone and his friends listened, I'd show my gifts, the pelts I hoped to exchange for his daughter. And I'd explain how the spirits had decided Down had to be both my woman and my pupil. I'd convince him eventually.

For now, we were in a situation over which I had no control. What was happening to me? Nothing in the life I'd led predicted dreams like those I'd had. Nor demands from a woman who claimed she'd died and come back to life, sharing her body with a Goddess.

I wasn't born into Stone's band. Nor was it Stone's band when I entered it. Before Grandfather Eagle dreamed of the new land, I'd been born the third son of Hawk Talon and the first child of his second wife, Thistle. My mother was killed by a great bear the summer after Beast Slayer visited our band. She died making time for me to run to safety. Small wonder I'd been so overwhelmed by our encounter with Bear Man.

Hawk Talon had loved my mother. He didn't want another woman, he wanted Thistle. Since she'd died to save me, he blamed me for her death. I was my father's bad luck. When we visited the annual spring gathering of The People at Lake Between the Mountains a few days later, my father traded me for a fine elk hide.

I was a runt and a favored target of bullies in my age group. But the man who bought me, whose name I never knew, must have seen something in me, some evidence of intelligence or shrewdness. He walked me around the lake to where the band of Stone's father, Bear Claw, had camped. Bear Claw's Spirit Man, Hears Voices, had recently lost the son he'd been training to follow in his profession. The boy had preferred hunting to dealing with spirits and never came back after setting out on a fine fall day, tracking the bloody trail of a moose he'd wounded.

Hears Voices asked me where I'd come from and why a stranger had bought me. Other questions, too, which simply puzzled me. I tried to answer honestly because I knew I was unwanted in my old band. Hears Voices finally led me into his tent, lit a fire, and sprinkled me with pollen. It made me sneeze but the Spirit Man didn't care. His daughter brought us a bowl of muddy water and Hears Voices told me to take it in my mouth, swirl it around, and spit it back in the container. Then he sat and stared at the contents of the bowl until I thought he might have fallen asleep. Finally, he raised his eyes and looked at me. "You'll do."

Hears Voices swapped me for his daughter. An even trade to the stranger who'd bought me. Trades like that were common enough. It was one of the ways The People brought new blood into their bands and enforced the laws against having children with relatives closer than cousins.

I never knew whether Hears Voices considered me a good investment. If he had second thoughts, he never told me. Nor did he ever indicate satisfaction with me. He immediately began teaching me about the spirits and I did my best to solve the riddles he used as his favorite teaching devices. I brought him the bad luck I'd carried from causing my mother's death. He died shortly after my vision quest and long before I learned most of what he planned to teach me. But I'd learned enough, barely, to satisfy Bear Claw, and then Stone, to keep my place inside their band.

I'd become Spirit Man for our band due to circumstance instead of a calling. But I quickly understood that my position as Hears Voices' trainee, and later as Spirit Man, made my size less important than my mind. I'd found myself in a band where the Spirit Man needed a new initiate. Then, too soon, a new Spirit Man. I was willing to become both because I'd been a boy who needed a purpose that made me worthy of a place in my new band.

Ever since Hears Voices died while I was only a teen, I'd spoken to the spirits for my people. And conveyed answers. Not answers I'd actually heard from spirits. Just what I'd learned the spirits would want if I could hear them. I was, in a sense, a fraud. Or had been until that morning when I first dreamed myself a skull. Before that, I'd never experienced anything like a real vision or revelation. Not even on my spirit quest.

The People believed that when a young man comes of age he should receive a dream telling him to visit the sacred mountain. Or, since the migration began, some other spot consecrated by the spirits. The boy went to his Spirit Man for guidance. The Spirit Man explained how the boy should prepare himself. Go away from the people. Not touch a girl or a woman. Not kill, even flies or mosquitoes. Recognize the holy place. Remain there for three days, eating no food.

If a boy did all that, the spirits sent his vision. After that, the boy became a man.

Other boys my age had already had their dreams. They'd come to learn from Hears Voices how to prepare themselves. Left on their quests. Come back to consult the Spirit Man and receive their secret names. I could tell Hears Voices was becoming concerned because I'd not had my own calling dream. I only dreamed of girls. Maybe they were my calling. In a way, I'd hoped so. Not that I shared that with Hears Voices. Finally, I told him I'd dreamed my calling. He instructed me, purified me, even gave me sacred herbs and told me to chew them if, by the third afternoon, no vision had come to me.

It didn't surprise me when that turned out to be the case. Especially when the wind stopped blowing shortly after I'd found my sacred place. By the third day the mosquitoes had nearly driven me mad. I broke that afternoon, slapping wildly at them, killing them in their hundreds, and painting myself with my own blood. I shouldn't have done that, but I hoped the herbs would save me.

They didn't. Even after I chewed them, nothing happened. I was crossing a stream on my way back the next morning when a raven scolded me from a nearby tree. My namesake mocked my failure, I thought. I'd been named Raven because I was quick and dark and had a sharp nose, and because my mother thought I had a clever mind. Not clever enough to leave this bird alone. I bent and picked up a stone and threw it at him. He screamed at me and dropped something as he lifted into the air. He circled for a moment as I went to look. As I searched for what he'd left, he crowned me with his excrement.

The other thing he'd dropped was a scrap of leather. A piece of fringe torn from a woman's skirt. That was as close as I came to a vision or a message from the spirits. When I saw how eagerly Hears Voices waited on me to share my experience, I invented an elaborate variation. It satisfied him. He gave me a secret name, but I'd decided my true secret name should be Visionless. At least until recently.

Did I deserve this? Were the spirits repaying me at last for years of falsehoods? I'd only tried to protect myself. To fit in. As Spirit Man, I'd never intentionally harmed anyone. But now, I had these strange dreams about a time long after my death. I also faced a demand from Willow, or The Earth Mother, sacred embodiment of The Goddess.

"You'll do what must be done," Willow said. She'd come up behind me as I sat on that flat rock. I hadn't heard her, but I'd felt a sudden chill and known she was near.

"What do you want of me?" I asked.

"First, my son offered you this." She held the little statue of herself I'd carved before I lost her, the one Bear Man had been wearing yesterday.

"I made that for you," I said. "Keep it, or give it back to Bear Man. I'm with another woman now. I may carve a different figurine."

She slipped the thing around her neck and tied it. "You already know what I want. You must extract vengeance on Tall Pine's killer."

"If I go back to the band," I said, "they may challenge and kill me. Stone is so angry, he might even challenge Down. It's the kind of extreme purification a mind like his finds easy to understand."

"Yes," she agreed. "But none of that matters anymore."

She stepped beside me and pointed down to the willows with her chin. Men boiled out of the brush and began climbing the slope toward us.

"You don't have to return to them, Raven. They've come for you."

Caught

"Our band has better trackers than I thought," I told Willow.

"Not really," she said. "Your dog went to get them about the time you fell asleep. He led them here."

"I don't believe that," I said. "Snow helped us get away. I can't imagine Snow intentionally betraying us."

"He didn't. I'm Goddess of the Animals. I sent him."

I didn't accept what she told me, but it made no difference. No matter how it happened, the men of our band were here. Stone would challenge and kill me. He might do the same to Down. At the least, he'd punish her severely. I stepped in front of Willow and looked back into her eyes. She didn't bother returning my gaze. Instead, she looked through me, at the men climbing the slope from the willows.

"Please protect Down," I begged her. "Don't let them take her unless you're sure she'll be safe. I'll turn myself over to them. They may satisfy their revenge on me."

Willow shook her head. "No. She'll go with you. I've told you where your duty lies. Now I'll persuade them to let you do it."

"How? Your band may be bigger, but it's mostly children and old people. They have more fighters than you."

Her eyes turned cold and deep as the river I'd lost her in. "We're prepared for them, Raven. Your life is safe enough...for today."

My reaction to her reassurance must have been clear.

"I know what's about to happen here." She finally looked directly at me. "I always know."

Her voice was so calm and certain that I briefly wondered if it could be true.

"Come with me," she said. "Let's talk to them."

She started down the slope. I thought about running back for my bow and arrows, but having them would only make it more likely that I'd be challenged—one at a time, if necessary, until they'd certainly kill me.

"Leave your spear." As if she'd read my mind. Reluctantly, I put it down and followed her.

The men of Stone's band, my band, formed a line to meet us. They strung bows and notched arrows as we came. They acted as if the two of us were a band of Enemies or dangerous beasts. With this new Willow, I thought, that second possibility might not be inaccurate. My Willow had been kind and sweet, so much like a less curious version of Down. But the gentle child I'd known had been replaced by a stranger, someone alien and dangerous.

"Oh, I am dangerous, Raven. More dangerous than you imagine." Her voice raised a nonexistent ruff along my backbone.

Willow held open hands up toward Stone and his men, palms out. "Put your weapons away," she said. She didn't raise her voice for them, but the breeze suddenly ceased and her solemn tone carried with total clarity. I could tell by the stunned look on Stone's face and the way the rest of the men turned to him to see what they should do.

"I am The Earth Mother," she said. "I've brought you to this sacred place. Your lives will be forfeit if you profane it. The man you've come for, Raven, is under my protection. I won't allow him to be harmed."

Stone's face twisted into a doubtful grin. "The Earth Mother," he shouted. "You lie. The Mother doesn't walk among us."

Willow's icy voice silenced him. "I do when I please. When you chased Raven yesterday, I sent a great bear to stop you. Today, I sent a dog to bring you here. As you see now, I've just called another bear to protect Raven."

Her hands waved in front of her, as if pulling something out of the empty air. Bear Man in his bear robe rose up from behind a tumble of lichen-mottled rocks a few strides from us. From my angle, it was apparent he was only a very large man beneath the huge beast's pelt. But I remembered how real he'd looked head on. The line of men fell back a few paces. He must have seemed real enough to them, too.

Stone's mouth moved, but nothing came out.

Finally, Takes Risks spoke. "What do you want from us?"

"There's been murder among you," Willow said. "It's an affront to the laws of The People. An insult to the spirits. It's unacceptable to me, The Mother, Goddess of Life and Fertility. A life I gave you ended before its time. The murderer must be found and punished. A life for a life. I've assigned the task of finding the murderer and returning harmony to Raven. I've rewarded him with the companionship of Down. These are my wishes and they shall not be thwarted. Raven and Down will return to your camp. You'll accept them as my spokespersons. They are not to be harmed. If they are, I'll smite your band—woman and child, man and dog. All of you will I smite until none remain and no other band shall ever speak of you again. Do you understand?"

Takes Risks whispered urgently in Stone's ear. Stone nodded and found his voice at last.

"We already asked Raven to rid us of our murderer. And thought he had. We apologize for our failure to understand, Mother. We'll do as you ask."

"I don't ask," Willow said. "I decree. I sense doubt, Stone. Resistance. Raven tried. Now he knows he was wrong and the killer remains to be found. I'm sending him back. And I'll send the great bear along to see that my instructions are obeyed. So your women and children won't flee in terror and so your men will understand my power, I'll send him, not in the form of a bear, but as a man." She gestured toward Bear Man. "Behold!"

A boy lay unseen in the rocks at Bear Man's feet. Bear Man threw the skin off and the boy hauled it down until it was hidden from the line of men below. To them, it must have seemed as if the beast had been instantly transformed. I heard moans of fear. Stone's eyes grew so wide I thought they might pop from their sockets. It was a great trick, but hardly spirit magic. Was that the way with everything Willow did? Had I only failed to discover the gimmicks behind the rest?

Bear Man stepped out of the rocks toward the men of my band. He rolled his shoulders and shook his head the way a bear might. He sniffed the air and showed them his antler club.

"Hello," he said. "You can call me Bear Man. I plan to see that The Mother is obeyed. While I'm doing that, I'll protect your band. But I'm hungry. You have brought meat, yes? Meat would make me happy. And you do want to keep me happy, don't you?"

They did.

◇◇◇

Bear Man went down to be feasted, offered nearly all the rations the men of our band had brought with them. Willow led me back up to the hidden camp, then took Down and me aside.

"You'll be safe enough for now. I'll send scouts to watch your camp. They'll let me know if problems arise. There's hardly any chance that will happen, but if it does I'll put in another appearance and reestablish the fear of The Goddess in any troublemakers."

"I thought you knew everything that's going to happen."

She gave me an icy look. "Close enough."

I nodded. A Goddess wouldn't need scouts. I noticed Down didn't seem awed by The Mother. That pleased and reassured me.

"For now," Willow said, "it would be wise not to mention the former members of your band who've come to join me. If any of the men recognized me as Willow, tell them the truth. That I am both Willow and The Mother. If they want more details, I'm sure you can create them, Raven, and make them believable. Down, you could do the same, but don't call attention to yourself. You're in less danger while they still think of you more as Stone's child than Raven's partner."

Down agreed and I didn't argue. In this, at least, I thought Willow was right.

"Raven, waste no time. Find the killer, prove it, arrange a confession in front of the band, then exact my revenge. When you're done, I'll reward you both. You'll have a son. Your band will never want for game as it travels south into the new country."

Down smiled. "The first of many sons and daughters, Raven."

"There must be one before there can be many," Willow said. "Now, gather your things and rejoin them. Return to your camp. Begin your work at once. This crime is a wound that might destroy your band and weaken The People if it's allowed to fester. Go heal it."

◇◇◇

Down and I stayed apart from the others on the walk back to our band's camp. Not that anyone threatened us, or even paid us special attention. They were focused on Bear Man. At first out of fear, then out of fascination. He told wild stories of his life as a bear. Many of them about his encounters with men who'd tried to kill him. And how he'd made them suffer. Gradually, our men began to ask him questions. The sex life of bears was of particular interest.

I stayed silent. My mind was focused on finding a way to satisfy Willow's instructions. Doing so seemed the best way of fitting ourselves back inside the band's structure—reestablishing roles that would prevent Stone and his friends from causing us problems later. But how?

Down finally interrupted my deliberations. "What will you do to find the killer?" she asked. "I was your first and most logical guess. Who's next?"

"I have no idea," I admitted. "How about you? Do you have any suggestions?"

She chewed on her lower lip as she followed the path through the willows. "Not really," she said. "If I had to guess, I'd say one of the women Tall Pine kept trying to couple with. One who refused and felt threatened, or one who let him have his way to keep someone else safe. A man she thought might lose a challenge if he found out, for example. Or, for that matter, a man who found out and didn't think he could win a challenge."

"Are there rumors of who that might be?"

"I think Tall Pine went after every young woman in the camp at one time or another. Add their men, and that's most of the band."

"What about Slender Reed?" I asked. That could be painful for Down to consider. Slender Reed and Hair on Fire had expected to become man and woman. I didn't think Slender Reed had been pleased at being given to Tall Pine instead. And she'd continued meeting Hair on Fire in the willows, competing with Down.

She shook her head. "Nothing for her to gain. My father would have given her to Bull Hump or Takes Risks…or kept her for himself after she bleeds again. At least that's what he's planning, if he can persuade Blue Flower."

We hadn't come up with a solution by the time we got back to camp. It looked peaceful enough as we descended the ridge toward the tents. Yet something was wrong. I caught up with Stone and put a hand on his shoulder, something I'd never have done before. He merely turned his attention toward me, and not his anger.

"Stone," I said, "you brought all the men with you, didn't you?" I suppose I already knew that, but I had enough troubles and hadn't felt in need of searching out more.

"I wasn't going to let you get away from us again."

"But that means you left the women and children unguarded."

He looked at me, puzzled.

"Where are our dogs?"

He swung around and faced the camp. "We brought many with us, but…"

"The others should be running out to meet us," I said. "The women should be calling greetings. But no one's here. Not unless they're hiding."

Stone let out a mighty bellow. It stopped the men where they stood. Stopped Bear Man in the middle of a story, too. Stone threw himself down the slope and began tearing open tent flaps. He howled Blue Flower's name. And then he bellowed even louder when he found some of the dogs dead inside one of our tents.

The men had stood in silence until then. As they realized their women and children were missing, they began shouting, too. And rushing down the stony slope, hoping they were wrong.

I grabbed Down and Bear Man. "Follow me. Let's circle around the camp. Find the raiders' trail. Even if the camp was hit right after the men left, no one could have taken our people very far."

Snow came with us. My best friend again. He showed particular interest in the rugged ridge at the other end of camp.

"Your dog's right," Bear Man said. I looked where he pointed and saw freshly disturbed rocks. Scuff marks, where a foot had slipped as they tried to climb up from our camp. Blood, even, where someone had fallen.

"But there's only tundra on the other side," I said. Arguing against the evidence before my eyes.

"They'll be harder to track across tundra," Bear Man said. "But while they're crossing it, they'll move slow."

He scrambled up the slope, using the power in his mighty legs to overcome its steepness. I had to climb at an angle and use one hand to help Down follow me.

"Can you see them?" I asked as the two of us joined Bear Man at the summit.

"How would I know?" That confused me until I looked across the rolling grassland on the other side. It was black with moving figures. Caribou, thousands, moving south. Bear Man shook his head. "The Mother makes this hard for us."

"Why would she do that?" Down said.

Because she's not The Mother and had nothing to do with it, I thought. Though I had to admit it felt as if someone were purposefully making life as difficult for us as possible. Instead, I called Stone as he desperately continued searching through the empty camp.

"Up here," I said. "They went this way. Bring everyone and all our weapons. No food. We'll be able to harvest what we need. And no dogs. Tie them so they can't follow us."

"There," Bear Man pointed. "That's where they left the ridge and started across the tundra."

I was in no mood to wait. I jogged down and began picking my way across the grass sedges. I'd only gone a few feet before I was assaulted. Mosquitoes—swarms so thick I could hardly breathe.

Yes. This would be as hard as The Mother could make it. The real Mother, I thought. Probably because she was angry with us for paying heed to Willow's claims.

◇◇◇

Our march across the tundra turned into a mindless slog. Our bodies were black with mud and streaked where perspiration washed away our protection from the mosquitoes. We hobbled, because of the sedge grass. We no longer talked to each other. Too many mosquitoes flew in our mouths and choked us when we tried.

The day had turned unnaturally calm and warm. Ideal for insects. Less so for us, and for the great herd that flowed around us, moving south. Moving the way we should be going if we hoped to find a suitable place to winter. But now *we* no longer existed, except as a hunting party. Our band had been broken, never to exist again unless we found our women and children and won them back.

I stumbled against the side of a caribou bull that hardly seemed to notice me. I hadn't realized he was there because we'd been swallowed up in thick fog. I paused and looked around for the others. Down paused, too, just behind me. She pointed and I picked out the towering form of Bear Man, and, less distinct though only a few paces beyond him, two other men I thought were Stone and Bull Hump. I couldn't see the rest.

Down cupped an ear and I realized I could hear voices. One sounded like Gentle Breeze, complaining. Were we nearing our destination? Or were the spirits playing tricks on us? I danced across the tussocks to catch Bear Man by the arm. I waved a hand at the mosquitoes swarming in front of my mouth and risked a whisper.

"Hear that?"

He nodded. "I think we're close." He reached out a long arm and tapped Stone on the shoulder with his club. Stone lost his balance and fell off a grass tussock, going knee-deep in the muck. He grabbed Bull Hump, pulling him over in the process. Bull Hump, I noticed, seemed to have forgotten the terrible pain of his wounded neck.

Bear Man shook his head at them and put a hand over his mouth. He cupped his ears and pointed ahead.

"I'm our best tracker." I only swallowed a couple of mosquitoes. "Gather the men while I go have a look."

Bear Man shook his head again. "Only if I go with you. The Mother made me responsible for you."

Too tired to argue, I helped him gather the men around Stone before the two of us faded into the fog. Three of us, I soon noticed, because Down hadn't obeyed me and waited with the men either.

Less than a bow shot from where we lost sight of our force, we topped a small rise and found a rocky, well-used path down to a riverbed. We heard the water before we saw it. White water, rushing down a steep decline from the mountains of ice. We were close to the glacier, though we could hardly see anything for the fog. Just above the river's chilled water, however, a cold breeze swept away the worst of the fog and most of the mosquitoes. That cold clear air revealed, far closer than I would have imagined, a village. The place was crowded with people, many of whom I recognized since they were the missing members of our band.

I signaled to Down and Bear Man and dropped behind the lip of the rise. "Enemies."

The village wasn't occupied by The People, except for the ones they'd stolen from us. The place belonged to another tribe. One with whom we'd sometimes fought and sometimes traded in the days before the migration began. Their tents had a different shape. Their clothes, a different look. Men and women let their hair grow long and braided and greased it. Woven into their braids were feathers and leaves and the occasional flower.

Our women and children seemed to be unharmed. They were being fed by Enemy women. And looked over by Enemy men. One large and very decorated fellow had taken a seat beside Blue Flower. He fed her from his own hands. I guessed she was about to become a headman's woman again.

Down poked me in the ribs and whispered, "Look." I followed her gaze and saw them—Walks Like Ox, Seven Fingers, and Crooked Nose.

"It didn't take them long to find a new home," I said, "or take their revenge on us." They didn't look as satisfied as they might, though. Probably because Down had been missing from the village. She was the one Walks Like Ox wanted for himself. He and his friends would have happily settled for Blue Flower, or some of the other pretty young women. But their new allies weren't sharing the bounty of this raid.

"Shall I go break a few heads and bring your women back?" Bear Man asked.

It was a big village. "You'd have to break a lot of heads," I said. "You could come help."

"All of us could help and I'm still not sure we can manage it. And some of our people will die."

Killing Enemies and killing People weren't the same thing. Still, even with surprise, there were so many Enemies that I believed we'd lose several of our men. We might even fail to recapture most of the women and children. "We need a better plan."

"Then you're in luck," Down said, "because I have one."

◇◇◇

Down wormed her way through the brush, crawling down the slope toward the camp below. We'd spread our men behind the lip of the river's bank. Their bows were strung. Their arrows handy. Spears lay nearby if needed.

I didn't like this plan. Willow had advised Down to keep a low profile until the men accepted her again. Instead, she'd taken the lead. Down would rescue our women and children and all would be forgiven. Or fail, and find everything blamed on her that had gone wrong since she broke The People's laws with me. In the end, I helped her persuade Stone and Bull Hump and Takes Risks to let her take this on because it might work. No one had a better idea.

The key was for her to enter their camp unseen. Once there, The Enemies wouldn't recognize her. The face of a strange young woman would cause no special concern. She must be one of the new captives, someone they hadn't noticed before. She could mix with our own women and children easily. Explain her plan. Get them to help her spread the word.

Down crawled to the place I'd pointed out. The Enemy's camp lay on an island across a narrow branch of the river. Down planned to cross to it behind one of their biggest tents. Just as she was ready to jump up and wade the stream, two Enemies, a man and a woman, slipped around the side of the tent to argue in private. They spoke a different language, not that we could hear them over the rush of the water, but I thought, from the way the woman shook her finger under the man's nose, that she objected to his plan to add one of our women to their family. They were very focused on each other, but if Down tried to wade the stream while they were there, they'd see her. A stranger sneaking into their camp wouldn't be the same as noticing her already among the other captives. We couldn't wait much longer. Some of the courtships were escalating fast. As soon as they started being consummated, our men would give vent to their rage. They'd rush down that slope, launching arrows and spears and angry shouts. The bloodletting would follow.

Down saw the couple but realized the need for haste. She slithered into the stream on her belly. I knew how painful that must be. The water was fresh ice melt, stealing her body heat in moments. She'd have to hurry across because the cold would begin weakening her immediately. She hardly disturbed the surface, keeping her body under water. Only her head remained exposed as her hands floated from rock to rock. She slipped once, but caught herself against the next rock downstream. She had to get out of the water very soon. Another slip could send her tumbling into the main current at the end of the island and The Enemy's camp. The water became much deeper there, and the flow far stronger. Watching her terrified me. Would I lose a second woman to the grasp of an icy river?

But luck, or the spirits, were with us. The young man shouted something at his woman and spun on his heel, worried that the captive woman he wanted might be claimed by someone else while they argued. His woman stood stunned for a moment before rushing after him. When she disappeared, Down stood. Even from where I waited, I could see how badly she trembled from the icy flow. She clawed out of the stream and disappeared into The Enemy camp. Would they wonder why she was wet? Or only admire soaked leathers clinging to the supple curves of her young body.

I worried until she found Scowl and Gentle Breeze. They wrapped Down in dry skins. Using emphatic gestures, she spoke and pointed.

Our time had run out. The large man who'd been feeding Blue Flower had grown impatient. He ordered two young men to help him. They held Blue Flower while the big one tore her leathers open and began shedding his leggings.

Stone rose to his feet, roaring. His arrow missed the big man, but struck one of those holding Blue Flower. The rest of us rose, too, launching more arrows. We had plenty of targets. Down ran toward the big man. She shouted, telling our women and children to run to us. While she ran, she aimed her drinking bladder at the Enemy Chief and squirted him. We'd filled the bladder with caribou blood instead of water. She screamed out The Enemy's word for "Menstrual blood!" Some of them tossed away polluted weapons. Others tore off fouled garments. Down bloodied the chief's sex. It immediately drooped.

Blue Flower broke free of the only man who still held her, joining the mass of women and children running in our direction. Down raced deeper into The Enemy camp, spraying caribou blood everywhere.

"Enough," I howled. "Come back."

She couldn't hear me, but she turned to see me gesturing, a proud smile on her face. Her grin twisted as an Enemy arrow slammed into her breast.

I threw myself down the slope like an enraged bull, looking for the man who'd shot her. Down staggered, but grabbed the feathered shaft with both hands and ripped it free. Her torso and belly were covered with blood. Caribou? Hers? I didn't know. I fired two arrows at Enemies as I sped toward Down. To my surprise, Enemy warriors fled from me. Because Bear Man was right behind. He terrified most of the Enemies, and swung his club, laying out everyone foolish enough to challenge us.

I tore Down's vest open and examined her wound. The stone point had been sharp. The edges of the wound weren't ragged and the arrowhead had hardly penetrated. It must have struck a rib.

"I'll be scarred," she said. "Will you still want me?"

I had to laugh. "I'd lie with you here and now if we weren't too busy. Is there much pain?"

"Enough." Her smile was half grimace. "But get me out of here someplace private and you can make me forget all about it."

I started to pick her up, to carry her from The Enemy camp to the relative safety of the ridge. She stopped me.

"No. I want them to see that their arrows can't even hurt The People's women."

"All right." I kept myself between her and more arrows. Bear Man followed, huge enough to cover both of us. The Enemies who hadn't fallen shouted insults, but they weren't following. Walks Like Ox and his friends were cowering and helping each other pull both sides' arrows from their flesh. I thought they'd be wise to run for it, if they could. They weren't likely to be as popular with The Enemy as when they'd delivered unguarded women and children.

We joined our reunited band. Down was the only member who'd been wounded. A minor wound, but it worried me. In the old times, when we fought The Enemy regularly, they were known to dip arrow points in their own feces to poison those they wounded. Down would have a scar. That was nothing. But if the tip had been poisoned...?

I did what I could to clean her wound, tying a poultice of chewed bark and herbs over the spot to stem the bleeding and reduce her pain. Bear Man did what Stone should have done, getting the band organized and marching back across the tundra to put distance between ourselves and The Enemies before they could sort themselves out.

The journey back was exhausting. But The Enemy didn't follow.

◇◇◇

Our camp lay just as we'd left it when we went after The Enemy raiders. Except for a little meat missing from our cache. A fox ran out of camp, his jaws filled and our tied dogs voicing their outrage. Our tents were mussed from The Enemies' struggle with our reluctant women and children. But no one else had raided us while we were gone.

I directed our men to loose the living dogs and carry the dead ones downstream. We found a place and piled rocks on them. I blessed them, purified those who helped me, and we went back to camp.

Our tents and tools and blankets were still there. Our beds remained, welcoming us. And we were all so exhausted we welcomed them as well.

Gentle Breeze refused to let me put Down in one of those beds. Not before she examined the wound and replaced my poultice with one of her own.

"Did you see the arrow?" Gentle Breeze asked me. "Was it tainted?"

"I pulled it out myself," Down murmured, "before Raven got to me. How would I know what was done to it? I tossed it away and ran for my life."

Gentle Breeze huffed a little, though she clearly felt as proud of Down as I.

"We'll keep a close eye on the wound, then. You know what to look for, Raven."

I did. When Gentle Breeze finally left us alone I didn't bother with taking Down back to the Women's tent. I didn't really believe her bleeding endangered us, but if it did, everyone already shared in that danger. I'd perform a purifying ceremony for the band tomorrow, after we slept. Most of the band was already sleeping. I pulled Down's bedding over beside mine, rearranged skins and robes and grasses so we had a comfortable place for both of us, then let myself lie beside her. I'd begun to drift off when Down's hand found me and she whispered in my ear. We stayed awake and active a little longer than the others in our tent.

Ice Eyes

Bone

The cold flames that normally flared along the hut's roof were dark. Thin, perfectly round, and straight branches the color of dirty snow hung up there in a way I couldn't fathom. This time, light glowed from a strange cone-shaped thing that stood on the flat wooden surface by my side. I couldn't figure that out, either. Not that I ever understood much in this alien place.

I glared at Ice Eyes. "Why have you brought me here again?"

Ice Eyes raised his head. He had trouble focusing on me. He sat against the wall across the hut from me, on an artificial seat. Like everything else, what he sat on had been crafted with a level of skill I couldn't imagine. Too perfect. Too even. Actually, I was beginning to find this continuous state of flawlessness boring.

"You're back," his voice said inside my mind. That made sense, I suppose, since I had no ears to hear. "I was beginning to think I imagined you."

"A dream imagines me—a fleshless skull that speaks?" I laughed to myself.

He joined me with a crooked grin.

"What am I, then, oh dream? The spirit that once inhabited this skull? That somehow haunts it still?"

"Damned if I know." He picked up another too perfect item from the floor beside him and lifted it in my direction. "Here's to you, ghost, or whatever you are."

He put the thing to his mouth and swallowed. It must have been a container.

"I'd offer you some of this but you've nothing to taste it with. And you probably aren't familiar with this kind of drink, anyway. Besides, you can't be real. I expect you're a product of my imagination. Or proof I've finally lost my mind."

"I might have said the same about you," I told him. "Or maybe you're hallucinating because you've drunk too much wine."

Ice Eyes looked at me, surprised and suddenly more alert. "You know about wine?"

"Of course. Though we don't have any now. The berries are just beginning to ripen and we haven't had time to stop and ferment any."

"Wine! In your time? Don't I wish I had proof of that. It'd make my career. Next, you'll be telling me you had bows and arrows."

"Yes, we *do* have bows and arrows. I shot Enemies, who tried to steal our women and children, with them today. My today, anyway. And my woman was shot. I'm worried about her wound."

He jumped to his feet and stumbled toward me. "War, wine, bows, tell me more. Tell me about your tools. Tell me how you live. Who makes decisions? Do you live with your father's people or your mother's? Do you have a god? Gods? Tell me everything."

"No." I stopped him dead in his tracks. "I need information, too. I need to make sure my woman's wound heals, if I get back to her again. Tell me how I got here. Where you found me. Are you a witch, planting these dreams in my mind? Or am I really dead as I talk to you here? And why should I believe anything you say?"

"If I try to answer your questions will you answer mine?"

I agreed, not sure I'd follow through. But I was desperate. Might Ice Eyes know how to keep Down safe? Did he know how I'd die? If I knew that, could I prevent it from happening? All those things, of course, mattered only if this were real. And surely it couldn't be.

He put a hand on his chin and looked thoughtful. I might have done the same if I'd had access to a hand.

"Well, for your woman who's wounded...I don't suppose you know about..."

Apparently I didn't. The word meant nothing to me and I told him so.

"I'm not a specialist in healing," he said, "but I know we grind grass seeds and bake the powder as one of our foods. When that food gets old, there's a thing that grows on it—a mold. You could use that to..."

"A healing mold?" I said. "We find various kinds on plants and berries."

"You know about such things then? That's even more remarkable than the wine."

"I know about molds. As does a woman in our band. If she has some or I can collect it, you're right. It could help heal my woman if her wound goes bad. I'll try that, when I go back again."

A chill raced down my non-existent spine as it occurred to me that I should have said "...if I go back again."

"Good," he said. "...should solve your first problem." Again, the word meant nothing, but the vision of the mold he knew was similar to ours. I'd treat Down with some if I could.

"Or," he continued, "if you can find some wine, pour it over the wound. The...should help cleanse it." Another word I didn't understand. It was the wrong time of year, but maybe one of the nearby bands still had wine. Or Willow. If anyone had wine, she would.

"And the bark of willow trees," he said. "I'm sure you know about that."

"I already treated her with willow bark. We have lots of that."

"Good," he said. "Your woman should be fine with all those treatments, unless the wound is too serious."

I assured him it wasn't.

"Now," he said, "let me tell you what little I know about how you came to be here. I am an...," he said. Still another meaningless word. I told him so.

He nodded. "When you camp in a place that's been used by others before you, have you noticed that old tools sometimes lie beneath the surface?"

"Of course. Broken ones that have been discarded, along with old bones, cracked for their marrow. Sometimes we even find worn out skins. And, once we dug a storage pit and found a grave. We had to close it and move and purify ourselves after that mistake."

"We have specialists who dig things up to learn about the people who were here before us. Some of us think that learning more about people like yours, who lived in ages before we came along, may help us understand ourselves. That's why my woman and I were invited here and how I found you."

Every hair on my body would have stood up as I considered what he'd said. "Are you telling me you found me...my skull...that you robbed my grave?"

"No, no," he said. "You were in a shrine. Just your skull, a few tools, this figurine, and...Say? Where's the figurine?"

"It was taken," I said. "I'll tell you who has it. But first, tell me about the shrine."

He did. Well enough for me to think it likely he spoke of Willow's cave. The Mother's cave. That meant, in my world, I might have very few days left to live. Or that I'd already died.

Who would build a shrine for me, anyway? Willow was the only one I could think of, though I had no idea why.

Unless Ice Eyes' story was part of some elaborate trick, I had to get away from there. If I woke again as flesh and not bone, I needed to put as much distance as possible between myself and Willow's cave as fast as I could.

"Who took the figurine?" Ice Eyes asked.

I tried to escape the question. I tried to make myself wake up back in Down's arms. Back in our camp. I couldn't manage it.

"Perfect Woman took it. She took it after you followed the other woman who got angry about finding the two of you together."

"Damn," he said. "I should have known that little…that she'd do something desperate to control me."

"Be careful of her," I told him. "She's willing to harm you much worse than that."

"I won't give her the chance," he said. He turned his back on me and stormed out of the chamber, leaving me alone in that terrible dream, trying desperately to wake from it and, just as desperately, to understand what it all meant.

Traps

I woke, briefly remembering only pleasant things. Like the joy I'd found in the girl against whose hip I lay. Then the skull dream flashed back into my consciousness and my eyes snapped open. It was late, our tent empty. Everyone else had already risen. Only Down still slept, snuggled beside me. And she was unnaturally warm. I pulled back our robes to cut away her bandage and poultice using one of my blades. The same blade had lain beside me as I talked to Ice Eyes. Hair rose on the back of my neck in a way it couldn't while I'd been in that dream. Down's wound had turned an angry red during the night. But at least no twisting lines crawled away from it just beneath her skin. The wound was infected, but maybe not badly.

Down hadn't wakened even as I removed her bandage. I covered the wound again, replaced her robes, and scrambled into my skins and boots. The inside of the tent had turned very cold. I grabbed an extra robe and went to find Gentle Breeze.

"He's awake." Scowl had been sitting beside the tent's flap, her duty to announce my rising to the band.

Low clouds raced across the sky, bumping and roiling, moving toward the mountains and ice like a stampeding sky herd.

Takes Risks jogged over to meet me. "Stone and Bull Hump have been talking with the men. They want you to arrange a purification ceremony immediately. We've shed blood. We've killed Enemies. Worse, our men have been in the presence of a woman during the time she bleeds. All these things put the band in grave danger."

I agreed. Especially since I felt in considerable danger myself. In danger of losing Down. In danger of losing my life. Of having my head spend an eternity in Willow's cave, waiting for Ice Eyes to find me.

"I'll arrange it. I'll need Gentle Breeze's help. Have you seen her?"

He pointed at another tent. "You'll find her there."

One of the boys had fallen yesterday as we scrambled up the rocks to get away from The Enemies' camp. Gentle Breeze was treating his scrapes and scratches, advising his mother.

"Stone and the others want a purification," I told her. "Will you help?"

She agreed.

"And I need you to look at Down. Her wound is infected. She has a fever. I think she needs a poultice with the healing mold. I don't have any left. Do you?"

Gentle Breeze shook her head. "I've been out of the mold for weeks. It's hard to find in this strange country and we spend so much time traveling. I've looked, but haven't seen any."

"Then, please do what you can for Down. After that, help me cleanse the women. As soon as we finish the women and I've purified you, search for mold. I'm afraid for Down's life, Gentle Breeze."

She chewed her lower lip and searched my eyes with her own. "We won't let anything bad happen to her. I'll find the mold."

Her concern was honest. She'd helped raise and train the girl. Gentle Breeze might not do this for my sake, but she would for Down's.

"I'll look at Down now," Gentle Breeze said.

I thanked her. "You've been a better healer than I am for a long time. Down needs you. And I desperately need Down to be well again."

Very desperately, very soon. Down would have to be healthy before the two of us could run away. But would Down run with me? I hadn't told her about my dreams. I certainly wouldn't tell Gentle Breeze. I wouldn't tell anyone in the band, except maybe Down. I'd thought of myself as a logical man, but talking of a dream gave it substance in the real world. I wouldn't hesitate to share most of my dreams with Down, but I wasn't sure about these. My normal dreams now usually involved Down and wonderful things we might do together. But losing my head—that was another matter.

◇◇◇

The band gathered everything we owned and carried it down the rocky path to the stream. I washed each item. Every tent, every tool, every blanket. I washed their clothing. And then I washed every member of our band, each time pausing to dust the person or item with a pinch of pollen, then a sweep with a grass brush I'd made for the occasion. As I did so, I chanted the words of purification.

It had snowed on us every few days that summer. Just when we needed it least, snow began falling again while I finished cleansing the last of our possessions. The band piled our supply of firewood and dried dung nearby and covered it while everyone huddled, naked, around the fires trying to stay warm and waiting for me. I stood at the edge of the water, stepping in and out of the ice melt. I'd wrapped my feet in a pair of boots I purified as soon as I purified myself. My feet were wet and aching from the cold, then numb stumps on which I stumbled about, unable to feel the ground beneath me. Great wet snowflakes struck me and melted until I shook so badly I could hardly manage to continue the ceremonies. As I worked and fought the brutal cold, I worried about Down. Bear Man carried her to me so I could purify her before anyone else. The cold air and water woke her and cooled her enough for her to smile at me and tell me she'd be fine.

Bear Man claimed bears couldn't become impure, not even when they assumed human form, as long as they acted on behalf of The Goddess.

"I'll be happy to continue looking after this amazing woman. I'll make sure she'll be all right."

I appreciated the offer but didn't think he could deliver on it.

He gathered up the Women's tent and its posts and carried Down back to the spot where it had been before Blue Flower found us. He built a small fire in the tent and took robes to wrap Down as soon as they dried.

I usually took extra pleasure in bathing and brushing the women, especially beauties like Blue Flower. This time I hardly noticed. Because I washed everything and everyone, it filled most of the day. I couldn't have finished if Gentle Breeze and Scowl hadn't begun heating water at the fires and using it to warm my poor feet. They brought me cleansed robes and rubbed me dry. At the end, too exhausted to eat, I found my way to the Women's tent and crept beneath the robes beside Down, letting my chill cool her fever and her fever warm my frozen body. Bear Man had built her a soft bed cushioned with thick grass he'd shaken out and dried. I was far too frozen and tired to feel it. Down clung to me, and I to her. I dropped into a deep and, thankfully, dreamless sleep.

◇◇◇

It felt as if I'd hardly slept at all when Bull Hump woke me, calling my name. I slipped from Down's side, crawled from the Women's tent, and joined him. The snow had stopped, but the clouds still hung, low and threatening. An icy wind wiped the sleep from my eyes.

"The men are gathering for a council. They want you there."

I sighed and drew a deep breath, searching inside myself for a hidden reserve of energy to get myself through this. I didn't find it.

"Raven," Bull Hump growled. "If you're fool enough to accuse me of being the murderer in front of the band, I'll slit your throat before you finish saying my name. No matter what the others do to me. Do you understand?"

I didn't. Was Bull Hump confessing? Or trying to scare me because he thought I might link him to Tall Pine's murder and accuse him in front of everyone? I felt old and tired, but I nodded and somehow followed him as he stomped back to the main camp.

The men had formed a circle in the center of the band's tents. Women and children huddled close behind them. I wondered if Stone or Takes Risks had decided to blame our fresh troubles on me. Bull Hump, at least, only worried about himself.

Could even Bear Man's presence or The Mother's commands keep me safe? Since I'd just slept in the Women's tent, would they require me to purify myself again? I'd have been frightened about what I might face, but I didn't have the energy for it.

No one remembered where I'd slept. Or they didn't care. Takes Risks recited our list of troubles, carefully mentioning my involvement in each. I warmed myself from the heat of the central fire and tried not to doze off. Takes Risks surprised me when he praised my role in the recovery of our women and children. He thanked me for the ceremony I'd performed before I slept.

"Raven," he asked, "what do you recommend we do next?"

I shook my head. Forced myself to think. "Move," I finally said. "This campsite has been unlucky. We need to get through the mountains before the seasons change. We need to follow the herds. We should start south as soon as possible."

The circle went eerily still. What I'd said made sense. Why hadn't anyone agreed?

Bear Man put an arm around my shoulder. "Raven, in your exhaustion, you forget The Mother's instructions."

The circle nodded and mumbled agreement.

"She said you must find the murderer," Stone said. "Otherwise, our band will be doomed. We may all die. And The People, every one of them, could suffer because of us."

Yes, she had said that. Just as she'd said Bear Man really was a bear. I'd been thinking, though not very clearly, of my own safety. I'd completely forgotten the commands of a Goddess I didn't believe in. Not Willow's version, anyway.

"And so," Stone continued, "we must stay here until you succeed. I think we'll let you rest today. But tomorrow, you will take up your task and all of us will cooperate. At the end of the day, you'll name the killer. Then we'll follow the animals again. Our band will have good fortune. Even if we spend a few more days here, The Mother will see that we make it through the mountains before the storms come."

I spread my arms, indicating the snow that covered the tundra as far as the eye could see. "What's this, then?" I asked. "I say it's a sign—winter's coming."

"This isn't the only snow of summer," Takes Risks reminded me. "I think, though you purified us, we remain unclean. There's one more cleansing you must perform before we'll be safe. You have to do what The Mother ordered."

"Yes," another spoke.

Every man in the circle expressed their agreement, and the women supported them. We weren't going anywhere. Not until I gave them a killer tomorrow. I could slip away, run on my own. But Down couldn't travel. Not with that wound. And I couldn't leave her. I was trapped.

◇◇◇

On my way back to the Women's tent, I ran into Gentle Breeze on the outside of the circle. I didn't have to ask about the mold. I could see in her face that she hadn't found any.

"I'm sorry, Raven," she said. "The snow covers everything. In this country, I don't even know where to start digging to look for it."

I nodded. I wouldn't do any better, brushing snow from unrecognizable plants. But I knew where to find the mold. The Mother would have some.

Walking from our camp on this ridge to the mountain and The Mother's cave, the last place on earth I wanted to go—if Ice Eyes had it right, the last place I would ever go—would take much longer than when I'd run there along stream beds with Down. The snow would be deepest among the willows. The dwarf trees slumped under its weight, hiding game trails. I'd have to cross the tundra, where the snow hid the edges of each sedge and the treacherous holes in the ice wedges that might lie in between. Walking across the tundra would be nearly impossible.

I went to Stone's tent, my usual tent, and found my skis. Not the elegant, long, smooth pieces of carved wood I learned on when we were back in the old country. I wore a pair of curved strips of mammoth ivory that endless exposure to heat and cold had caused to flake off from the remains of once elegant tusks. With the help of my spear to push myself across the flat spots and give me balance, they'd do.

Bear Man stuck his head in the tent. When he saw me tying my feet inside the ivory, he understood.

"You're going to The Mother to get help for the girl, aren't you? I'll borrow some skis and come with you. Make sure you're safe."

Make sure I wasn't running away, I thought, but I didn't say it. Instead, I told him, "You can't. You have to stay to insure that Down's safe. Besides, you're too big for any of the skis we have."

"What's this about skis?" Takes Risks entered, overcrowding the tent.

"He's going to The Mother's cave," Bear Man explained.

"Down needs a special medicine," I said. "We don't have any. In this snow, we can't find it, either. But The Mother will have some."

Takes Risks rubbed his chin. "The snow may melt before you get back."

"Or it may not," I said. "Even if it does, I'd have to search for the plants on which the medicine grows. It could take days. Down may not have days, and all of you want me to solve the murder tomorrow."

"That's true," Takes Risks said. "And you're right. Bear Man is too big for our skis. He's more valuable here, protecting our camp. I'll go with you."

He kicked through the piles of robes and equipment I'd purified. No one had sorted our things and stored them neatly. His favorite skis were bigger and smoother than mine. Better quality because he got to choose before me.

"You could stay here, Raven," Takes Risks said. "You need the rest. It's obvious how much you need it. Explain to me what you want and I'll get it from The Mother."

"She may take some persuading." I had to go in person in case I needed to remind Willow she had to send some back with me if she wanted me to stay and find the murderer.

Takes Risks didn't argue. He stuffed an extra robe and his bow and arrows in a pack and threw it over his shoulder. He grabbed his spear and pushed open the tent flap. "I'll tell Stone and get us some pemmican. Then I'll meet you on the ridge above camp."

I would have thanked him, but he was another part of the trap that held me. Not that I planned to run, but I hardly wanted company as I went back to the cave where Ice Eyes said my skull would spend eternity.

◇◇◇

Takes Risks didn't talk much as we skied into the wind. He pointed out the tracks of predators when we came near them. Made sure I stayed alert to the possibility of meeting the creatures that made those tracks as we picked our way around groves of snow-bowed willows. Otherwise, he left me to my thoughts and seemed deep in his own.

I concentrated on sliding one foot ahead of the other. It was all I could manage.

"We're not alone," Takes Risks told me as we neared The Mother's cave. "There," he pointed at a pair of men paralleling us on the other side of the creek. "And behind the rocks above."

I didn't pick them all out. They didn't concern me. The Mother, Willow, would want to know ahead of time whenever anyone came to visit her cave. I uncovered my head, though the wind embraced me with a cruelty that made my face ache. That way, they'd know who approached. I heard bird calls from the willows and the rocks. Not from birds because they'd huddle in their nests and ignore us in weather like this. The old man, Mammoth Rider, Bear Man's father, trotted down the slope to greet us.

"The Mother bids you welcome," he told us, "but thinks you haven't yet completed your task, Raven. She would have preferred you to finish before you came here again."

"I would have preferred not to come at all," I said, "but I must speak to her."

"Of course. She waits for you. Perhaps your companion would like to join us beside the fire. We have warm stew."

We hadn't paused to snack on the pemmican we'd brought on our trek to The Mother's cave, so Takes Risks accepted with enthusiasm. He had ambitions, but he believed The Mother possessed great magical skills. Magic, operating under different rules than men like Takes Risks understood, was something he preferred to avoid.

I followed the old man. The Mother sat in the corner she'd occupied when we were last here. Her eyes stared into the rock across from her. Or through it. The old man didn't say a word as he turned and left me with her. I waited a few moments until, overcome by impatience, I spoke.

"Willow. I need something from you."

Her eyes blinked. Once, twice, three times. She slowly turned to face me.

"The healing mold. Yes. I already sent it. And a small bladder of wine. Gentle Breeze has them by now and Down will respond to her treatment quickly."

"Your spies told you? Then why didn't they tell me? Save me this trek across the tundra?"

"Because I decided I should see you. To remind you of your duty and to suggest you stop avoiding it. We no longer have much time to repair this."

That took me aback. "What do you mean?" I demanded, wondering if my skull would leave this place in its current functional condition even once more.

"We, each of us, have our allotted time. You're old, Raven. You know your days are numbered. Mine, too, since I'm nearly as old as you and only part of me can survive beyond a normal span of years. This body I've borrowed can't."

I breathed again. I'd thought she might be on the verge of talking to me about my dreams. I couldn't decide whether there really was something magical about this woman I'd known so well many years before. Or whether her strangeness came as a result of nearly dying in that distant river.

At that moment, Willow suddenly looked at me out of The Mother's eyes. A wistful look I hadn't seen in this new Willow, but one I recognized from our youth at times when she was troubled.

"Oh, Raven," she said. "You should sleep. But you can't, can you?"

She reached into her robes and pulled out a piece of pemmican.

"Eat this," she said.

If I was going to eat, I'd prefer the stew, but I didn't argue. I only wanted to turn around and hurry back to Down. I bit off a piece. It had a strange flavor.

"This will ease your aches and give you some energy—for a while at least."

To my surprise, it seemed to help almost immediately.

She took my hand in both of hers, the way she used to, and backed toward the cave's opening. "Come with me, Raven. I want to show you something."

Her voice sounded young and excited. Her smile told me she expected to surprise me with something wonderful. She'd done this once when she led me to a flower unlike any I'd ever seen. Soft and pink and nearly as beautiful as the young girl who showed it to me.

This time, she led me out of the cave, her pace quick and girlish. She almost skipped up the path. I couldn't help but smile as she dragged me behind her. We followed a twisting trail that snaked across and up the side of the mountain. I had to trot to keep up with her.

And then she stopped and turned and smiled at me again. "I loved you very much, Raven. But we both have different partners now. We can't go back, but it was sweet that you wouldn't mate with Down when you saw me watching. Thank you for that."

It had been The Mother's aspect more than Willow's, but I didn't correct her.

"I have a surprise. Cover your eyes." That was like her. She'd reveal it in her most dramatic fashion, as she used to when we were young and in love. Once, when I uncovered my eyes,

Willow waited, naked and willing. So young, then. So beautiful. Did she remember that moment?

I covered my eyes. I should have worried, as she led me up the path and around a corner. There might be some terrible drop this new Willow planned to shove me over. But I was with the old Willow now. For the moment, I trusted her absolutely.

A cold wind struck, so we'd come around a bend in the trail. That nearly made me peek, but she didn't give me enough time.

"Now." She pulled my hands away from my eyes.

We were higher than I'd thought and near the edge of a dangerous cliff. But that wasn't what she wanted to show me. Below us, from horizon to horizon, the earth moved. Not the earth, of course. Because what moved was brown and beige and tan and shaggy and the earth lay still beneath a cover of trampled snow.

The mammoths were the first animals I identified. A dozen of them, some with frolicking calves. And mastodons. Their pace seemed slow but purposeful. They moved in the middle of a tremendous mass of caribou. Further from the base of the mountain were horses. Nearly as many as the caribou. And bison. Elk, too, and moose and ox. All the great animals. They filled the earth. Why didn't I feel the mountain shake with the weight of their passage?

Here and there, bright spots of snow stood out. In them, predators paced among the herd animals. Lions, tigers, bears, wolves, wolverines. They flowed toward the mountains and the ice, all of them together, as if some temporary truce had been struck so they might all successfully reach the land that had been promised us.

"Amazing!" I breathed. I had never seen so many animals at one time in one place. I probably never would again.

"Isn't it?" Willow squeezed my hand. "Aren't they magnificent?"

"Yes."

"Our allies. They share the world with us. They compete with us and make us better, stronger, and wiser. They feed us, clothe us, provide tools and weapons. And they teach us not to take them for granted. They show us that life is as precious to them as it is to us."

Willow shook her head. "We need, them, Raven. The part of me who's The Mother believes we'll come to waste them. Fail to revere them. That we'll worship our wealth and comfort at their expense. That part of me believes we're here, now, because this place is one of the last on Earth where the great herds will prosper in abundance."

She turned and took my hands in hers. "But there'll come a time when even this place is threatened. The Mother dreams. She traveled to a time when many of the beasts you see below us will have vanished. When we might stand on this spot and not see a single animal."

"Surely not."

"No, it's true. I shared The Mother's dreams."

"What else did she dream of?"

Willow shrugged. "You know. You've had troubling dreams, too, Raven."

"Was she…were you a skull?"

A small tear brimmed in the corner of Willow's eye. "Yes. A skull. Someone carried The Mother and me to this spot and showed us where this tundra used to be. I don't know how to describe it. It was almost unrecognizable, and there were no animals."

I reached up and wiped the tear away, peering deep in those familiar eyes. "It's only you right now, isn't it Willow? The Mother's gone."

"She's always here, Raven. But she's given me control of our body for this conversation. She knows you don't believe she saved my body and shares it with me. So, for now, though she hears, it's I, only Willow who speaks."

"Can't you keep her out?"

Willow smiled. For the first time since we left the cave I saw the wrinkles in her face. She had aged, though not so much as me. Her face had become more weathered and fuller. Still attractive, but the texture of her skin had hardened from when I'd known her.

"Raven, I don't want to keep her out. She's The Mother. Our Mother. The Earth Goddess. And she saved me when I died. She isn't evil, only…only pragmatic. She does what she must for the Earth's good. For the animals' good. Her children's good, and we are among her children."

It didn't matter whether Willow truly had become one with The Mother or simply believed something that wasn't true. I honored The Mother, and believed in her. I believed in a Goddess who cared about every life she allowed to end, but who didn't interfere in them.

"Raven," Willow said. "She asks me to tell you that she does care, but sometimes has no choice but to interfere. Each life is precious to her. That's why, when life ends, she guides its soul to the stars to join with the spirits of the dead. And then, sees that it's born again. She says she could force you to believe in us, the two of us in this one body, if she wanted, but that she allows her children to accept her or not, as they wish. She promises you'll always have that option, though she hopes you'll keep an open mind about our union."

I looked deep in Willow's eyes again. No hint of the mother stared back at me.

"I'm trying."

"Good. Now, we need to go back to the cave. There's more she wants me to show you."

Would she show me how I'd die? Where my skull would rest? But I didn't think so. If it were something as cruel as that, I reassured myself, my Willow didn't know it yet.

◇◇◇

Willow took me back to the cave. Takes Risks saw us coming and raised an eyebrow, obviously wondering if it were time to leave. I shook my head and followed Willow. She guided me to the deepest corner of the cave. A heavy robe hung against the stone wall there, weighted along a jutting seam at its top by rocks the size of my skull, not that I had any reason to compare things in that way.

It was pitch black behind the robe. Willow pulled it aside and I saw rocks and a wolf's skull on the floor. The wolf's skull chilled me. I felt sure it occupied the spot where Ice Eyes would find me.

"The Mother usually keeps the figurine you carved of me beside the wolf's skull," Willow said.

Yes. I would replace the wolf.

The world whirled, as if my head might come off and roll to its predetermined spot just in front of my feet. I nearly pitched over against the cavern's walls before Willow steadied me.

"Are you all right? Do you need more pemmican?"

I closed my eyes and concentrated on steadying my feet and breathing. When I finally found my voice, I told her I was fine. But I ate the last of the pemmican, hoping it might help.

"Be careful and stay right behind me," she told me. "Our path follows a narrow seam through the rock here. The floor is uneven and it twists and turns. Hold my hand and I'll lead you."

"Why not bring a torch?"

"We never bring torches in here, and we won't need one. Trust me."

I managed to avoid stepping on the wolf, in its role as temporary substitute for my skull, and followed Willow into the crevasse. Narrow hardly described it. We twisted left, then right, making headway only a few feet at a time. I barely kept my feet under me. Then the walls grew wider and I realized I could see. Not much, to begin with. Only Willow's dim outline revealed itself in front of me at first. Was there another entrance? As the light became brighter, I could tell it flickered.

"You're wasting wood or dung, keeping a fire going in here when there's no one to see it."

"Wait." She led me deeper still.

We emerged into a large, domed chamber, not that I could see the roof clearly. The fire that illuminated the place was tiny and the cavity was huge—and surprisingly warm.

"Look at the fire," Willow said. "Tell me what it consumes."

I looked closer and discovered it consumed nothing. There were no logs, sticks, dried dung…nothing. It danced and wavered above a small crack in a great stone. I bent closer still and reassured myself that I could feel its heat.

"Is the fire underneath, or does the rock burn?"

"Neither." She pulled her robe off her shoulders and swung it through the air. "Watch."

She dropped her robe over the flame and we stood in total darkness. I heard her pull the garment aside but the flame didn't reappear.

"Give me your hand," she commanded.

I did and she held it over the hot stone.

"Feel that? Not the heat, the breeze."

I hadn't noticed until she mentioned it. "Yes. I feel it."

"That's what burns—the breeze, the mountain's breath. The earth itself breathes through the crack in this stone. Now watch. I brought a piece of flint with me. See how I restart the fire."

I saw the sparks walk across the stone. There was a tiny boom as if a clap of thunder had just been born and voiced its first complaint. The sound was accompanied by a flash that momentarily reached far above us, nearly to the distant ceiling. Then only the little flame danced along the fracture in the rock again.

"My man, Mammoth Rider, found this place. A band of his people lived in this country then. Hardly anyone else. The main entrance to this cave was higher up the slope than the one we use now. It opened on the view I showed you—the place where we saw the animals.

"Mammoth Rider's band thought it would be a perfect place to camp. They could watch the herds and protect themselves from the weather. His band celebrated their find by collecting wood for a great fire just inside the cave's mouth. They planned to roast a pair of freshly killed caribou and rejoice over finding such an ideal place for their new home. The young men gathered dead willows by the stream and carried them up the mountain. Mammoth Rider tried to outdo all the others. He gathered wood until his arms were completely filled. Then, as he started up the mountain, it exploded like a volcano."

"A volcano?"

She nodded. "You remember the mountains that smoked. We passed them on our way toward the new land. Mammoth Rider tells me it was like those explosions, but different. The fire didn't tear off the top of the mountain. It blasted out from the mouth of the cave. Mammoth Rider dropped his wood and ran up the trail. He passed a smaller cave that had also exploded and set fire to the brush that had masked it. That's the entrance to the cave our band uses now. The opening to the larger cave disappeared in the explosion. Part of the mountain fell and sealed it. He called and searched, but none of his band survived.

Eventually, he explored the little cave. He found the crevice that leads to this chamber. And discovered the small fire that burns here now.

"You see, Raven. The roof here extended above the mouth of the cave. The breeze that seeps from this crack is made of something that burns. Whatever it is, it floats on the air the way a stick floats on a stream. Over time, the mountain's breath had gathered above us. Above the place his people lit their fire. You saw how, when I relit the flame, it briefly became so much larger, reaching for the roof. Mammoth Rider thinks the air up there had filled with the mountain's breath. The Mother says it's a special gift from Grandmother Earth, but that we're not yet ready to receive it. She's not certain we'll ever be ready. For now, we keep this passage secret and see that this flame continues burning, so the breeze from inside the Earth can't build up in this cavern again and destroy some other band who might happen on it.

"When my body dies, The Mother plans to have the entrance to this cave sealed and to bury me just inside, like the wolf's skull—a warning to her people that they must not go beyond that spot."

"That won't happen for a very long time, Willow."

"It will come when it comes, Raven. You know that. The Mother is in no hurry to do without me, but she's begun arranging what must be done when my time here ends."

"Thank you for sharing this sacred place with me. Or shouldn't I thank you? Doesn't The Mother have a purpose for me here as well?"

"I'm sorry, Raven. I'm afraid your dreams have already answered that question. And it's why The Mother wants you and your band to be brought back into harmony with the Earth and the spirits, and into The Mother's Way. Accomplishing that is part of why you must find and punish the murderer before tomorrow ends."

Somehow, she knew the deadline Stone had set me. And I'd been right about the wolf's skull at the entrance to this place. "I see," I told Willow. And I did. But that didn't mean I had to like it. Or even to let it happen.

Questions Without Answers

Takes Risks didn't seem interested in what had happened between The Mother and me. He didn't even ask if I'd gotten what we came for. Still, he was more talkative on our return trip. Just as well, since the effects of Willow's pemmican soon began to wear off. A deep, aching exhaustion nearly persuaded me to lie down and curl into a ball and sleep right there in the middle of the tundra. Sleep until I froze, or until something came along and ate me. Takes Risks kept me going by giving me things to think about. He kept me moving and made my mind stretch to understand what he had to say.

"You know, Raven, Stone hasn't been an effective leader. It might be best for all of us if your investigation discovers he's the killer."

I had to ski a dozen strides before I realized Takes Risks thought the person I accused and punished didn't have to be guilty. Whoever murdered Tall Pine was a secondary issue as far as Takes Risks was concerned. Might that be because he'd done it or expected to be the one who'd replace Stone? Stone had persuaded the band to back him after his father died because the old man had led them successfully for many years. Stone's size and strength reinforced the idea, especially when he didn't turn out to be as wise as his father. The size and strength of the three men he surrounded himself with helped him maintain his position. Now, one of them, Tall Pine, was dead. Would Bull Hump support Takes Risks, or would he want the role of band chief for himself? All I knew was Bull Hump had no intention of letting me accuse him. Takes Risks was the smartest of the three who remained. Or, at least, the cleverest and most creative. Would our men prefer Bull Hump the bully or Takes Risks the devious? Takes Risks had just proved his skill to me by suggesting something outrageous and making it sound like no suggestion at all.

What if Stone really was the killer? Would the band select one of his supporters to replace him? Might they select someone else all together? Someone less threatening, say? And, if the band did that, how would that man rule if Bull Hump and Takes Risks combined against him? I didn't know. Exhaustion engulfed me like a growing avalanche. I understood what Takes Risks said, but I couldn't wrap my mind around what might happen if I took his suggestion.

"And Bull Hump... How do we know he didn't stick that arrow in his own neck just to avoid suspicion? Maybe the two of them, together..."

It would be so much more convenient if I eliminated both the men Takes Risks perceived as rivals.

"I want you to know," he continued, "I'll support you, even if you discover reasons to challenge someone in authority. In fact, if I should become headman, I'd want you beside me as my main adviser. You'd be second in the band only to me."

Well, that was interesting. But what, I wondered foggily, if I accused all three of the crime? Would the men of the band let me go that far? Not that the three were guilty. I felt all but certain of that. But how bizarre a decision would the band let me get away with? Would they accept it because my choice might make us more likely to succeed, even if I let the murderer continue to live among us? And what of Willow? In her role of The Mother, I knew she wouldn't let me get it intentionally wrong. Or would she...if my decision coincided with an outcome she wanted? Would even The Mother let me bend justice? Or could I fool her?

Just before Takes Risks, still rambling about the wonderful life I'd have as his second in command, led us up the ridge toward where our camp lay, a warm wind rolled across the tundra. The snow, already mushy from hours of sunlight, began melting almost immediately. Takes Risks and I removed our snow masks and our skis because the path we had to climb led up a steep slope. The stone would be as slippery wet as when covered by snow, but it would no longer accommodate our skis. I got mine off, but wouldn't have managed to get back up that slope if Bear Man hadn't come bounding down the trail. He picked me up, grabbed my things, and set off in the direction of the Women's tent.

"Don't forget what I said," Takes Risks reminded me as Bear Man's long strides separated us. Unlike his name, Takes Risks didn't take the risk of following us to the Women's tent.

I nodded, lacking the strength to answer.

"Down?" I asked Bear Man.

"Much better," he rumbled. "The Mother sent healing powder and wine. Gentle Breeze said washing the wound with wine might make things worse. So she and Down drank it. But Gentle Breeze made a new poultice with The Mother's powder. Come and see for yourself."

He lowered me to the ground in front of the tent and Down opened the flap for me. Her eyes were clearer, though they flooded with worry when she saw me. I must have looked even more than my accumulated years. As old as death, perhaps.

Down took me in her arms. Her skin felt warm, but it was no longer flushed with the fever she'd had. Ice Eyes had been right about the mold at least. It had begun to work its miracle.

"Let me see your wound?" I said. Or maybe I only tried to say it. Down started untying the strings that fastened my clothing instead of hers. I tried to protest, but I can't remember speaking. Down told me later I was asleep before she managed to remove my skins and tuck me between our robes.

◇◇◇

Bone

I was in Ice Eyes' hut again. He wasn't there. The strips of cold flame were dark, the way they'd been last time. The cone-shaped light still glowed. The wine container stood on the floor where it had before I woke from my last dream of being in this strange and terrible place—just before Scowl alerted the band and I spoke to our council. That seemed so long ago in my world. So much had happened to me while only moments passed in Ice Eyes' world.

I sat on that slab of wood and waited for what seemed a very long time. Finally, Ice Eyes returned. "The little bitch got back to her people before I could catch her. Then my woman chewed me up and spat me out. She yelled at me all the way back up here. In front of everyone. What a piece of crap this day turned into." He cursed after that, using words I thought must be exaggerations.

What did he mean by everyone? I'd only seen Ice Eyes, Perfect Woman, and Second Woman. I tried to use my new vision that let me see beyond the range of normal eyes. Apparently it had limits. I could see nothing past the interior of this hut. I had a sense of other places and more people, but it was vague and uncertain. It didn't matter, I decided. Other things did. I needed to know more.

"How far are we from where you found me?" I asked. "From where you uncovered me with your digging?"

Ice Eyes mumbled to himself and took another drink from his container. A long one, tipping it back until it was empty. He wobbled a little as he bent and opened a small but all too perfectly angled door. He removed another container exactly like the one he'd emptied, twisted the top off, and sipped from its mouth.

"How far?" I said again.

"What? Oh, sorry. Deep in my own troubles. They must seem like nothing to you, considering. But, where I found you? It's not far. We're just outside the cave. You were at the back of the main chamber at the beginning of a passage that had been filled with rock and earth."

"Show me."

"What?"

"Take me out of here and show me the exact spot where you found me. Let me see this cave. I think I know it in my own time. But I have to be certain."

"All right," he said, "why not?"

I held my breath. Well, not really, of course, having no way to do that. I was bursting with terror and excitement. What if I hadn't been found in Willow's cave? What if this was some other mountain and my future still reached toward an unknown destination? On the other hand, what he was about to show me might confirm my worst fears. If he took me where I expected, death and I would soon meet and my soul's final resting place stood all too near where I hoped my living body still lay beside Down's.

Ice Eyes carried me out of what I'd thought was a hut. I suppose it was, but I'd thought the space I'd been in was all of it. That wasn't true. Ice Eyes took me into a tunnel inside a bigger structure. A perfect tunnel. What else? We passed openings that led off of it, the kind of exact rectangles I'd become accustomed to seeing Ice Eyes and the others pass through to reach the place where I'd first dreamed myself a skull. Ice Eyes stumbled past these, then put a hand on a rectangle at the tunnel's end. He grabbed a round projection and twisted. The thing opened on bright daylight glowing off the face of a cliff only paces away.

"Over here." Ice Eyes pointed at a narrow opening in the cliff wall. The sun seemed hazy, our shadows not sharply defined. I looked up and discovered an eerie yellow sky across which a silver bird few high and fast. It was no bird I knew. It didn't move its wings and they trailed smoke, as if its feathers burned.

A strange fog hung over everything. Still, the mountain's rock had a duskier hue. There were no lichens to cover it with color. The cave's opening seemed different, too. Its outline wasn't like The Mother's cave I remembered. I felt a brief surge of hope as Ice Eyes bent and carried me inside.

Mysterious lights dotted the walls. They shone down on the floor as if aimed. Trenches crisscrossed the space, making it unrecognizable. A flat stone lay at the bottom of one by the far wall. Its shape was identical to the stone on which I'd seen the wolf skull as Willow led me to the hidden chamber. That rock hadn't been artificially shaped like everything Ice Eyes and his people made. It was natural, and thus, unusually flat and oddly circular…unlikely to be duplicated in nature.

"There," Ice Eyes said. "On that rock. Your skull was surrounded by a handful of stream-rounded cobbles, all of similar sizes and bright colors. I found the figurine, face up, propped so that its head lay in your right eye socket. The rocks formed a pattern. I can show you what they looked like if you want. Maybe you can tell me what that means. Oh, and you faced the opening to the cave, looking out."

I wasn't interested in the rocks. "I see. Take me back outside. Let me look at the mountain. Let me see the tundra and the horizons."

"Whatever."

We went outside, exiting in front of the hut. Behind it should be the mountains and the ice. I couldn't see them because the hut stood too close. The ground under us was perfectly flat and gray. Absolutely even. At the cave's entrance there was stone and dirt—rocky, irregular, without grass. No mosses or bushes or lichens—just stones and earth.

"If this is the place I remember," I said, "there should be a path that circles up and around the mountain to our left."

"Yeah. Nice view up there."

The path was more or less where I remembered. It curved gently around and up, ever steeper. Like the ground between the huts, its rugged stone surface had been replaced by one that was smooth and gray. Every few feet a perfectly squared step took us higher. Someone had bordered the path with a wall that curved along what I assumed must be the edge. The wall rose, absolutely smooth, and high enough to block my view of the tundra. But far, far away, I saw mountains.

Were they those I'd known? I wasn't sure. In my time they'd been snow- or ice-capped. And brilliantly verdant in summer, which it must be since the sun shone and Ice Eyes hadn't put on heavier clothing and still seemed warm enough. Where, I wondered, were the mosquitoes?

At last, we came to the place where the trail ended. Where Willow had told me Mammoth Rider's people once built a great fire in the mouth of the wrong cave. Over all the years I must have lain within, the shape of the mountain's face had changed little. And yet it felt completely different. Rocks must have tumbled. Vegetation had died. Where I remembered flowers and berry thickets and lush greenery, now only occasional clumps of wispy, dry grass reached, without enthusiasm, toward the ugly sky. I glanced over the edge toward the tundra and my jaw dropped. Or would have, if hadn't lost that, too.

I had no idea what I was seeing. Beginning directly below and extending nearly as high as where we stood were…huts? Artificial constructions, but monstrous ones.

When tundra lay down there, I'd have seen angular shapes in the ice wedges. Since we came to this country, I'd known the ice sometimes mocked rare items found in the earth. Like the crystal in my medicine pouch, ice could also be multi-sided. The ice wedges and my crystal were natural, but no two were exactly alike. What had been built at this place mocked nature. It consisted of squares and rectangles, many identical and all connected to one side or the other of a staggered rectangle, like limbs upon a tree, except this thing clearly wasn't alive and never had been.

"What is that monstrosity?"

"It's the central facility." Ice Eyes sounded proud. "It connects production to separation facilities and the pumping station."

None of that made any sense to me. I told him so.

"Look." He gestured beyond the structure.

I did, and was more horrified still. Out where I'd expected tundra lay a dry and dusty landscape. Completely alien. The sedges were gone. There were no animals. Nothing but long, snake-like things, many of them standing on legs that lifted them to connect to Ice Eyes' central facility at a variety of levels. The snakes crawled everywhere across the landscape. And then I realized what Ice Eyes wanted me to see. There were more strange and terrible constructions out there. Some were much like the thing below me. Others stood like solitary towering pine trees, narrower at the top but many times taller than any pine tree I'd ever seen. All these unnatural things were connected to each other by snakes—a few big enough around to hold a man.

"Holy Mother!" I gasped. "What is all this? What are those snake-like things?"

"It's funny you should use that particular expression. Some of our people still pray to a mother, though I think they're addressing a different woman. What mother are you speaking of?"

Ice Eyes might be drunk, but he hadn't forgotten his profession.

"Soon," I said. "First, tell me…well, start with the snakes." Snakes was the wrong word, of course. Like everything in this awful world they were artificial—too perfect to be alive.

He tried, using words without meaning.

"Simpler. Start again"

"Under all this land there are great pools of…" He paused, trying to think of a way to describe the stuff to me. I saw it in his mind. And recognized it.

"The shining liquid that floats on water and makes it undrinkable?"

"Yes," he said. "Sometimes it's liquid. Sometimes it's…" He stopped again, deciding how to explain. "People eat things that make them break wind."

"Of course," I replied, frustrated that he'd changed the subject. Before I could try to get him back on the topic, he went on and I began to understand.

"Have you ever seen that wind burn?"

When the people were very hungry, an animal's carcass might be thrown directly on the fire to cook before it was butchered. I'd seen such carcasses bloat, heard the eruption of their wind. It did burn, quite dramatically.

"Yes," I said.

"Well," he continued, "our lives are based on that liquid, or a liquefied version of its wind-like form. We burn it, to light and keep our homes comfortable. We make things with it. What you call snakes are hollow tubes, empty on the inside like water reeds. We force that liquid through them. Use it, or send it to others in trade for things they make that we find useful."

He stepped nearer the edge and again waved the hand that wasn't holding me. "As far as we know, this is the last place on Earth where that liquid can still be extracted. Amazing, isn't it?"

He sensed how greatly I despised what he showed me. "I suppose the world has changed a great deal since you lived."

"It has." I felt like gesturing, too, like pointing at the tundra. Instead, I directed his view inside my mind. "What happened to the tundra? Where did it go? Where are the ice wedges? Where are the animals? The great herds? The mosquitoes?" I made him see it all, including how this same place had looked when Willow showed it to me filled with living creatures. Then I let him see how The People lived in harmony with the Earth. I recalled all his questions about our life and gave him answers.

"Oh my!" Ice Eyes said, obviously as shaken by the abundance of life in my world as I was by its absence in his. "There's been an awful cost for all of this, hasn't there?"

"Where did it all go?" I demanded.

"Our people sprayed a plant killer on this land before we developed it. Of course, it stopped being a tundra long before that. It's a lot warmer here now. Has been for ages. Can you feel the heat? Maybe you can't, but see how I'm sweating. It's not because this slope is all that steep."

Suddenly, I felt the awful heat. Smelled the acrid stench of dead air. "I don't understand. You killed all the sedge grasses? The willows? The animals? Why?"

"Not me. I didn't do it. It was…what would you call them? A clan that specializes in that liquid, I suppose. The woman you call perfect, it's her clan. Of course the tundra changed long before they sprayed. Even in your time, this land never got much precipitation. What it got it kept, stored as ice and frozen earth. Lakes and streams and mud in summer, just above ice that never melted. Eventually, all the ice did melt and this turned into a grassland. Still some wildlife, but none of the great herds you remember."

I made myself look at the land instead of the huts and snakes. The streams were gone. Where there had been lakes in which I might once have bathed or fished, there were only low spots where the sparse clumps of grass grew a little thicker.

"A long time ago," he said, "we fought a war a very long way from here. Some people thought we'd win more easily if they destroyed the plants so The Enemy wouldn't have a place to hide. It didn't quite work out, but since then we've improved our abilities. When they built this place, dug down to those pools in the earth and connected our snakes, they sprayed so nothing whatsoever grew here. Now, some scruffy grass does. And a little cactus. They'll probably spray again soon. We can't have dry brush around or we might have wildfires. That's way too dangerous."

"What happened to the animals?"

"Change. People. There are a more of us on the Earth now than in your time. Maybe a thousand of us for every one of you. There are still lots of animals, but no wild herds, really. I know you had domesticated animals. Did you plant seeds?"

"Some people carry seeds from one place to another so a favorite fruit or berry might grow where they move."

"Well," Ice Eyes said. "We deal with our herds a little like your people handled those seeds. We grow them where we want them, in controlled spaces. We harvest them to feed ourselves. There aren't many wild animals left."

"How did you persuade The Mother to allow this? Why hasn't she swept your kind from the face of the Earth?"

"The Mother? Oh, you mean the woman represented by your figurine. Mother Nature, we call her. We beat her, or tamed her a little. We have more control over nature than you did."

"What? You tell the wind when to blow, the rain where to fall? You have no floods or storms? The Earth no longer shakes beneath your feet?"

Ice Eyes shook his head. "Not that much control. I'm sorry. Ours isn't a world you'd want to live in, for all the fine artifacts and comforts we provide. You know, now I'm not sure it's a world I want to live in either. Especially since you showed me…"

He paused, rubbed his chin, thinking. "Actually, that's why I do what I do. To know what it was like and teach my people to appreciate your kind and your world. How you lived. How you suffered. How you died. Because knowing that might encourage my people to question how we live, I may have trouble telling your story. The perfect woman and her clan own all this. She's been trying to persuade me to be quiet about you. If she has her way, your skull and tools and that beautiful figurine will end up in a private collection where hardly anyone sees them."

"So I'll exist in a world without herds or hunters or prey? Where The Mother, who keeps us all in harmony, no longer exists? You're saying I'll spend eternity as a skull on display to perfect people who won't understand I was once a living, breathing man with wants and needs? Separated from the woman I love? I'd rather die!"

I laughed. I'd rather die? That seemed to be exactly when my troubles would begin.

Journey to a Confession

I slept for a very long time. They tried to wake me over and over, or so I discovered later. They couldn't. I didn't respond. Down finally persuaded them to leave me alone. To let me rest, but she worried about me.

I wonder if my spirit was away from my body then, temporarily lost in that terrible, distant future. Or had exhaustion simply overwhelmed me? Were my dreams the creations of a damaged mind, or messages from the spirits that I couldn't properly understand?

I finally woke when Stone came and shook me by the shoulders. "Raven, come quick," he said. "I need to show you something."

I struggled to untangle my mind and sort my dreams from reality. "Down?" I asked, confused. Shouldn't she be in the tent with me?

"She's up and around already. And much better. The last I saw her, she was asking Gentle Breeze how to wake you. You slept through the night and three-quarters of a day. But you've got to come with me now. It's important."

The sun was dropping toward the hills behind which it hid for a longer time every night. My bladder was full. I stepped to the edge of the ridge and emptied it. Then gathered my robes and spear and followed Stone.

"This way." He led me away from camp to a game trail that cut down a steep slope toward the water.

"What is it?" I asked. "Where are we going?"

"Not much farther," he said. "Right in the brush over there." He pointed away from the trail to a spot where bushes and dwarf willows had created a nearly impassable patch. "Only a few steps in there."

"What am I looking for?"

Stone shook his head. "I want you to see this for yourself. Then you tell me what it is."

Very mysterious. And why would Stone come get me, and only me, to identify something for him?

The brush tried to snag my leathers, but I could see from crushed leaves and broken branches that someone had been there before. I began checking the ground ahead of me, trying to determine where this makeshift path ended.

Stone put one hand on my shoulder and pointed with the other. "See it? Down there by the stream."

I looked where he was pointing. Other than a sudden drop just a pace in front of me, all I saw were willows, water, grass, and rocks. Nothing unusual.

I shook my head. "I don't see it."

"Lean forward a little," he said. "I'll hold you."

The drop was just a step in front of me. Who knew how solid this footing might be? To my right stood a short, thick willow, solidly rooted on the slope. I took a step toward it and grabbed a thick branch, thinking I could use it for support if I needed to lean over the edge. As I stepped, Stone suddenly pushed against the shoulder he'd been holding. I lost my balance and jumped for the heart of the willow. I didn't make it. My feet went out from under me and I found myself dangling over a drop of what must have been five times my height.

I turned toward Stone for help. His arms waved as he tried to keep his balance. I thought he must have tripped and grabbed at me to keep from falling. Except I was no longer there. As I watched in horror, he toppled over the edge. For an instant, he hung there, eyes wide with surprise, mouth open, uttering a very un-Stone-like shriek.

The drop sloped slightly out toward the stream. Just enough for him to strike it head-first before he tumbled to flat ground a few paces short of the water.

I kicked and grabbed and finally got my other hand on a solid branch and pulled myself back into the thicket. "Stone," I called. "Are you all right?"

Stupid question. I knew he couldn't be all right, but I hoped he'd answer, that at least he still lived.

I got no reply. From what I could tell, he wasn't moving. He wasn't lying at a natural angle. One of his legs was broken. I could see no safe way down to him from that spot, so I scrambled back over to the path and descended as fast as I could. I tore through the willows and found him, to my surprise, still breathing. Wheezing, actually, through bloody bubbles. I might be a skilled healer, but his injuries appeared beyond my ability to mend. With Gentle Breeze's help, maybe we could save him. I wondered if he'd want to live as a cripple. Perhaps Willow—The Mother—might provide some miracle if we could get to her in time.

That would be a problem because I couldn't even carry him back up the slope to the camp by myself. I bent and put my face next to his. To my surprise, his eyes were open. They even focused on me.

"How'd you know?"

I could hardly hear him.

"Know what?"

"Know there was nothing to see?" he whispered. "Know it was a trap? Know to step aside just as I pushed you?"

"You pushed me?" My response wasn't a clever technique for getting at the truth. I was bewildered, numbed by what he'd said. All I could manage was to repeat his words back at him.

"Had to have you out of the way before you named the killer. You'd be too important, then. But dead this afternoon, you don't matter. I can sell Down. Oh my, what a price he offered."

"Sell Down?" I echoed. That got me to focus. "To whom? Who offered to buy her?"

But his eyes lost their focus and drifted shut. He still breathed, but he'd lost consciousness.

I wasn't sure I wanted to help him after what he'd said. But I certainly wanted to keep him alive long enough to tell me more. The person who wanted to buy Down might be willing to kill me so he could have her more easily. And maybe he wanted me dead because he'd killed Tall Pine.

I checked Stone over quickly, to be sure he wasn't bleeding too badly. There was plenty of blood, but none had pooled and none spurted.

"I'm going for help," I told Stone, even though I didn't think he could hear me. I turned and sprinted for the trail and camp.

◇◇◇

I'd hoped Down would be back at the Women's tent so I could tell her about her father in private, then send her for help while I went back to deal with his injuries. She still hadn't returned. I slowed to a fast walk before I entered camp. I'm not sure why, but I didn't want to arouse curiosity, especially when my explanation would likely start a panic. Stone needed help, not hysterics.

Unlike me, our band had lost its desire to beat the change of seasons and match our migration to that of the animals. People sat about in front of their tents. Women cooked and chatted amiably while mothers watched their children play. Some of the older women sewed torn clothing or robes. Men knapped spear and arrow points. The place had the feel of a permanent camp, calm and lazy, with no concern that I had to solve a murder and announce the guilty person's name when the council met at day's end. But people's eyes followed me, relieved whenever I passed them without asking questions or making accusations.

Bear Man backed out of a tent on the far side of the fire. My tent, usually. He was one of the people whose help I needed. He heard me as I approached him and turned to me. "Hey!," he said, startled. "I'm surprised to see you."

I supposed everyone had decided I'd sleep forever. I'd have been satisfied just to sleep past the night's council meeting.

I stepped in close and kept my voice low. I told him what had happened and asked if he knew where Down and Gentle Breeze were. He didn't, but he offered to see if he could carry Stone up from the streambed. Or, at least, make sure no predators happened along to make matters worse.

"Just let me grab my club," he said. "Get what you need to treat him, and find the women if you can. I'll either meet you on the way back, or at the spot where he fell."

I couldn't think past finding my healing kit and telling Down and Gentle Breeze. Bear Man ducked back in the tent. I started to follow, then remembered I'd left my healing materials in the Women's tent.

Scowl sat on the far side of the fire, mending a tear in a robe. "Down was with Gentle Breeze, last I saw her," the old woman said. "But then Gentle Breeze ran into that tent over there a few minutes ago. One of the boys cut himself on his father's spear."

I thanked her and found Gentle Breeze in the tent Scowl had indicated. I bent and whispered Stone's needs in her ear.

"Look at all this blood," Gentle Breeze told me. "This child nearly cut off his finger. I've got to get the bleeding under control before I can help you with anything else."

I hadn't noticed the blood or been aware of the hysteria inside the tent. I wasn't at my best just then.

"Come when you can." She nodded. "Do you know where I can find Down?"

"She should be back at the Women's tent soon, looking to take care of you."

That was where I needed to go for my healing supplies. "Hurry if you're able," I told her, and then headed back the way I'd come.

Down still hadn't returned. I found my healing pouch under a muddy pair of moccasins, tossed them aside, grabbed the pouch, and ran out of the tent. Straight into Bear Man.

"You don't need that pouch anymore," he said, "but you do need to come look at the body."

He led the way.

Stone wasn't where I'd left him. He lay at the edge of the stream, facedown in the edge of the water. His legs and torso sprawled on the bank. And one arm. The other, like his face-down head, floated in the icy creek.

"What?" I said, completely puzzled. I thought Bear Man must have carried Stone to the water to let him drink or maybe to wash his wounds. But why leave his head in the stream?

I ran to Stone and plunged my hands in the water, grabbed his hair, and pulled his face into the air. Stone had turned gray.

"Why'd you leave him like this?" I whispered.

"I found him like this," Bear Man said.

I didn't believe what I'd heard. "Like this?"

"Exactly like this, except I pulled his head out of the water, like you, long enough to be sure he was dead."

"There's a gash on the back of Stone's head that wasn't there before. And I left him over there." I gestured at the spot below the clump of bushes and managed to lose my hold on Stone's hair. His face splashed back into the water.

"Leave him," Bear Man said. "He won't mind anymore. Come look over here."

I stood, but didn't follow him as he went to the foot of the drop. "I don't think Stone could have crawled here. He was too badly hurt."

"Raven, someone moved him these last few feet. They bashed his head. See this stone and the blood on it. Then they made doubly sure by leaving him facedown in the stream. You have another murder to solve."

◇◇◇

"Could an Enemy have done this?" I asked Bear Man.

"No," he said. "Look here."

The bank of the little stream was stony and covered with vegetation. But a few muddy spots showed moccasin prints. Just the front part of a foot, as if whoever made them struggled to lift a heavy weight. Stone's body, I supposed. The prints were small, a boy's or a woman's. There weren't any complete prints.

"Notice anything unusual in the pattern of the stitching?"

I didn't at first. The style of the moccasins was what I'd expect of any member of our band. But Bear Man proved a better tracker than I. Or less emotional and calmer in his observations. He pointed at one of the prints. I hadn't noticed, but when I looked carefully, just the hint of the stitching between the upper and lower halves showed along a muddy edge.

"A small foot," I said. "And it seems we should look for a moccasin with a twist in the stitching near the ball of the right foot."

"Exactly," Bear Man said. "Now come up and look at the spot where he fell."

We went back to the trail, then scrambled across the slope.

"See?" Bear Man said.

A long, straight willow branch stretched between two smaller clumps of brush. It had been cut on both ends, though the leaves had been left along the shaft to disguise it. The middle was cracked, where Stone's feet must have been caught by it. The ends were still firmly woven into the brush on either side. The trap had been set at the right height to trip a man looking somewhere else, as Stone had encouraged me.

"He didn't need that. He could have just pushed me." Actually, I remembered, Stone had pushed me, but not until I'd grabbed the adjacent willow and tried to use it to pull myself around for a better look at what Stone wanted to show me.

Bear Man knelt, looking at the crushed plants and disturbed earth. "You must have just managed to clear it when you jumped. And look at the crack in this limb. You're lucky it didn't break and drop you down there beside him."

I didn't feel lucky. Stone had tried to kill me. And now someone had killed Stone. The same person who killed Tall Pine? This was complicated. How was I supposed to solve it in just a few hours?

"What should we do, Raven? Carry him up to camp? Go get Takes Risks and Bull Hump and let them see this for themselves? Or should we see if we can find that moccasin?"

I remembered the muddy moccasins in the Women's tent. For some reason, I didn't mention them to Bear Man.

So close, I told myself. So very close. If only I hadn't overslept. If I'd woken and discovered Down, fit enough to leave the tent on her own. If I'd thought fast enough, the two of us might have slipped out of camp together. Run for the pass through the glaciers and the mountains. Run from The Mother and her cave. Saved ourselves, if only…

Now, my other plan probably couldn't succeed. Or could it…?

Bear Man interrupted my frantic thoughts.

"Let's see who's in camp and who isn't. Maybe examine a few moccasins."

"All right," I said. Why not? That way I didn't have to make a decision yet. Maybe a little more time would let me find a way out of this.

"We can't take long, though," Bear Man said. "Stone's not on any of the main trails, but he's close to camp. Someone will find him soon."

"Look for Takes Risks and Bull Hump," I told him. "I'll find Blue Flower and check her moccasins—look at as many women's feet as I can." And, of course, I'd try to find Down.

◇◇◇

I went back to the Women's tent first. No Down. No one else, either. But the muddy moccasins lay beside the tent's open flap, not far from the bed Down and I usually occupied. One had a twisted leather binding at the ball of the foot. A match to the tracks beside Stone's body. The moccasins seemed a little big for Down, and I felt sure I'd have remembered that twisted strap if she'd worn this pair before. I picked up the moccasins and began to stuff them inside my jerkin.

"You found the moccasins," Bear Man said.

I must have looked guilty.

"I wasn't following you," he said. "I thought maybe you'd found Down and she could help us decided what to do."

I showed him the moccasins, "But they're not Down's," I said.

"Whose, then? No one else has been using this tent."

Gentle Breeze had spent time here treating Down's wound. Some of the other women had probably brought food or come to try and help. But only someone who'd been beside Stone's body, probably his killer, could have brought them here and left them. Only one person I could think of seemed likely to have done that. And so I panicked.

"Bear Man," I said. "I confess. I killed him. I led him into those bushes and them jumped out of the way and made him trip. I killed Tall Pine, too. It was me. I'm the murderer."

Facts and Fictions

Bear Man stood, looking at me and considering what I'd just confessed. He was silent for what seemed a very long time. "I suppose you could have," he finally said. "And borrowed Down's moccasins to shift the blame to her, except you wouldn't want to do that."

He thought again for a moment, and then his eyes lit. "Ah," he sighed. "I understand. You found the moccasins and now you think Down killed her father. Maybe the other one, too. So, by confessing, you're trying to save her."

I denied it. "Oh no," I said, "I killed them." But he had at least part of it right.

I'd thought at first that Down killed Tall Pine in self-defense. But since I'd gotten to know her better, I believed her denial. My heart told me she wasn't a murderer. But what would the band think with her father dead and the moccasins that left prints by his body now lying among our things in the Women's tent? They'd be sure she did it, unless she could prove she'd been somewhere else this time. I didn't know about that. I was terrified the band might declare her guilty of killing Tall Pine and maybe Stone, too. Because I had no idea who'd killed Tall Pine, the only way I could keep her safe was by persuading the band I'd done it.

"Really, Bear Man," I told him again. "I'm the killer."

Bear Man continued to stand there, shaking his head.

"Look," I said. "I'm going to gather the men for our council now. I'll confess, explain what I've done, and they can decide how to punish me. The Mother has a purpose for Down. Remember? So you mustn't say anything to make them suspect her."

I started out of the tent but Bear Man stopped me.

"Don't rush into something stupid, Raven. The band won't believe you killed Tall Pine. Your confession may make them more likely to convict Down."

He took the moccasins I'd found and examined them carefully. Then he studied the ground around the entrance to the Women's tent.

"These made the prints down below. But look. They haven't made any here. See, there…and there. These prints are smaller and the stitching is finer and without twists. They must be Down's prints."

He was right. There were hardly any other prints in the Women's tent except mine. The ones he pointed out had to be Down's.

"Still," Bear Man mused, "that doesn't explain why you found the ones with the twisted lace here. Smaller feet, already wearing moccasins, might slip inside these larger ones."

My head whirled. I'd thought she'd killed one man to protect herself. But I couldn't imagine her killing her crippled father so savagely. And neither could Bear Man, though he kept finding reasons to wonder aloud if, just maybe…

"Let's start at the beginning, Raven. Tell me why you're so sure Down killed Tall Pine."

"She didn't," I said. "I did it."

"You weren't there when Tall Pine died," Bear Man said. "You couldn't have killed him or seen Down do it, because you'd scouted ahead of your band. When Tall Pine died, you were camped along the stream where you later killed the mammoth."

"I sneaked in during the night. Then I ran back to where I'd camped so no one would know I'd been there."

"Raven, The Mother has had you watched for a long time now." He sighed loudly. "I myself watched you sleep that night. I followed you. Watched you climb that ridge to get away from the lion I scared off. You saw me in the willows. I know you only made one trip to the camp and couldn't have killed Tall

Pine. Down is unlikely to have killed him, either. She'd have had to take him completely by surprise because he was so much stronger. Why are you so sure she did it?"

"I'm not sure." I desperately tried to change course. "What if, at the council, I declare someone else did it? Someone who'd be no great loss to our band? Someone who values his own desires over The People's needs?"

Bear Man shook his head. "You couldn't condemn an innocent man. You may think you could to save Down, but I don't believe it. It won't matter anyway because I can't let you lie to Mother."

My head sunk to my chest. How could I save Down?

"What if Down killed Tall Pine but had no choice?" I said. "What if she did it to save herself or someone else?"

"Mother already told me Tall Pine was murdered in cold blood. That there was no self-defense, no effort to protect another."

"I know Tall Pine tried to assault Down at least twice. He'd asked Stone for her as soon as she bled. Tall Pine threatened Down. Said he'd kill Hair on Fire if she didn't give herself to him willingly."

"She told you that?"

Actually, she had. "I have eyes and ears. I kept watch on her. And on Tall Pine."

"You've explained why she had a reason to kill Tall Pine. Not why you're sure she did it."

"I'm not sure, Bear Man. I believe she's innocent, but I'm afraid the band won't agree."

"Tell me, have you ever asked Down if she killed Tall Pine? Did she confess to you?"

"Of course I asked her. And she didn't confess because she didn't do it."

"Well," Bear Man said. "Let's find Down. We need to know where she's been today. I want to judge her denial for myself."

We didn't have to find Down. She came around the tent from the direction of camp, carrying something wrapped in a robe.

"What denial?" she said.

Bear Man had the good sense to look embarrassed. I just looked stupid.

"Whatever it is," she said, "it can wait a moment."

Down hugged me with her free hand, obviously feeling much stronger.

"I'm glad you're finally awake," she said. "I thought if I made you a treat, I might tempt you into waking up. I'm sorry there isn't enough for Bear Man, too."

Bear Man didn't seem to want to look at her. He obviously wasn't ready to confront her. He fumbled with the moccasins, absentmindedly tying their laces together before he shoved them in his belt.

Down unwrapped one of the precious wooden bowls we'd carried into this treeless country, casting the robe that covered it aside. She'd found ripe snowberries, probably on a south-facing slope where they'd gotten more sun than the bushes I'd seen. She'd crushed them and mixed them with snow rescued from a north-facing slope. This was a treat our people made for children. I remembered Gentle Breeze making it for me a few times when she was my woman and we were hardly more than children ourselves.

Down's pleasure at surprising me this way gleamed in her eyes. This happy girl couldn't have just killed her father.

Bear Man ran a massive finger along one side of the bowl, sucked it clean, and made an appreciative sound.

"No more," Down scolded. "Poor Raven needs a pleasant surprise for a change."

Bear Man nodded. "Especially today." He looked from her to me. "I'm sorry, but we're running out of time." He turned back to Down. "Why did you kill Tall Pine?"

Her jaw dropped. "What makes you ask that?"

"Raven just confessed to killing Tall Pine, even though I know he wasn't there when it happened. He's saying it to protect you because he thinks the band will believe you're the killer."

"You're certain Raven couldn't have done it?" Down seemed relieved. "You're absolutely sure?"

Bear Man nodded. "Mother had me watching the place Raven camped that night. He left early because he didn't sleep well. I followed until he returned after Tall Pine was already dead."

Down looked at me. "I'm so glad. I've always been a little afraid you did it to protect me, Raven. Tall Pine was killed with that garrote you made, after all."

"Bear Man," I said. "You watched me that night. Did anyone from your band watch our camp? Could someone have seen what happened?"

He shook his head. "The Mother would have told me."

Down put a hand on my arm. "Eat your snowberries before everything melts. You're going to need your strength and your wits when you face the band tonight. I know you'll find a way to make the real murderer confess."

"But we can't prove you didn't do it, and I'm afraid we may have to do that," I said and noticed Bear Man nod.

"What about today?" Bear Man asked. "Can anyone tell us where you've been?"

"Gentle Breeze saw me. But that's been awhile. I've been gathering berries and snow. Why should I need to prove that?"

"And how about these moccasins?" He showed her the ones with the twisted lace. "Are they yours?"

She shook her head. "What's going on?"

"Your father was murdered," Bear Man said. "Killed near the creek not long ago. We left him there because I thought we needed to clear up this confusion between you and Raven about who killed Tall Pine. Then I hoped there'd be no doubt where you've been today."

Down's eyes had gotten very wide. "Who'd kill him and why? Was he robbed?"

Bear Man and I exchanged glances. We hadn't checked.

"You're right," I said. "Bear Man and I didn't search as thoroughly as we should."

"Show him to me," Down said. "I know what he carries."

Before I could lead us from the tent, Gentle Breeze's voice howled from down near the stream. We were too late.

◇◇◇

Stone's Woman, Blue Flower, seemed inconsolable. Otherwise, it appeared the band's ceremonial wailing was more frightened and angry than mournful. We wasted no time getting Stone in the ground. Bear Man and I had touched his body. So we prepared him and performed the necessary rituals. Then we found a spot in a rockfall several hundred paces along the ridge downstream from camp. After we planted him, I purified us and Blue Flower, whose assistance had been necessary.

When we finished, the men called us to the council. Bear Man and I joined their circle. Down stood behind us among the women. She didn't need to keep herself away from the men anymore. She'd stopped bleeding after she was wounded. Her time had been briefer than normal, but she was young and Gentle Breeze and I agreed the infection might have interrupted her cycle. When some members of the band objected to Down's presence, Gentle Breeze confirmed Down no longer bled. I'd purified her since the bleeding. Her presence wasn't a threat to men or their weapons and tools. At least, not until trickster moon winked her way back to Down's next cycle.

Just as we got that settled and people again took their places around the circle, The Mother arrived. Her spies really must keep a close eye on us. She walked up to the men's circle, told two of them to make room for her, and sat where no woman had dared before. I smiled when no one challenged her. But only for a moment. A very good chance remained that my skull would soon take its place in the cave and begin waiting for Ice Eyes to find it. And Down might be joining me.

"Well, Willow." I made no mention of her claim to be The Earth Mother, "I gather your spies told you we've had another murder. Did they tell you who committed it?"

"No. Only that it happened."

If I could diminish her in front of the band, I thought it would make Down and me a little safer. But Willow didn't cooperate.

"My people," she continued, "didn't see the murder take place. Not that it matters. I know who the murderer is. But it's not my duty to cleanse The People or your band. The task is yours, Raven. I'm here to help you concentrate on it."

We sat, quiet, for longer than was comfortable. I looked around the circle and discovered most of the men looking as confused as I felt. The reason suddenly struck me. Our band leader ran these meetings and he lay under a pile of rocks, waiting for the scavengers that were sure to visit his grave.

I stood and stepped into the circle. "We must elect a new headman. Should we do that now, or, since I'm the one Willow tasked with solving the first crime—now this one, too, I suppose—would you like me to direct this gathering?"

"Yes," I heard one say. "Let Raven proceed."

"The murders first," another agreed. "They take priority."

"Does anyone object?"

The circle and the women remained silent.

"All right. You know we've just lost our leader." I explained how he'd taken me above the stream to show me something. Told them he'd fallen, though I left out how he'd tried to kill me. Reported where Stone had been when I left to get help and how Bear Man found him only moments later. Stated how it appeared Stone, though already crippled, had then been struck on the head and moved to the water's edge, left facedown in the stream to insure he wouldn't survive.

"And you remember his friend—our first murder victim. How someone strangled him with a sinew thong in the middle of the night. Two murders. Two terrible wounds to our band that do us great damage and could deeply injure all The People."

"Three," The Mother said. "The boy with the red hair who died trying to kill the mammoth. Though not murdered directly, his death didn't come by chance."

Hair on Fire, too? Who was The Mother accusing now? This addition to the deadly crimes I was to solve shocked me so severely that I nearly spoke Hair on Fire's name in front of everyone. Not a good time to remind them of my tendency to scorn tribal rules.

"Hair…," I blurted. "Er, the boy with red hair was murdered?" I faced Willow. "Why didn't you say so sooner? You could've told me when you asked me to find the first killer."

"It's the same killer, every time. Only one act of vengeance is required for all three."

That eliminated most of the people I'd thought might be guilty. It probably eliminated me, since everyone knew where I'd been during the killing of the mammoth. But it left Down. This sudden need to explain away a third death flooded me with anger.

"If that's true, then why such a rush now? Why not then?"

"Because the killer will act again soon. Very soon. Unless you prevent it."

"Willow, what are you saying? Do you mean unless we, the band, prevent it, or unless I prevent it? Will the killer act because I name people who might have done these deeds? I thought I knew who killed the first man. I was wrong, and I know that person couldn't have been responsible for harming the boy with red hair or our headman."

"Are you sure?" Willow's voice had gone deep and cold like the river where we lost her. I felt the chill of her words walk up my spine. Involuntarily, I raised my eyes and scanned the women until I found Down. Yes, I thought. I'm sure.

"Tell us who you suspected, Raven." Willow demanded. "Let your people hear your suspicions. Let them weigh the words of the accused and share what they know of these matters. Let the band decide."

"No. You told me *I* must solve this. Let me do it in my own way." I looked into Down's eyes, willing her to turn and slip out of the crowd. And then run.

She met my stare and shook her head, as if she understood what I wanted her to do. Or, as if she couldn't believe I still had doubts about her.

I'd have to go through my suspects, one by one. Hope to catch someone in a lie. But before I began, Bear Man spoke.

156 J. M. Hayes

"Raven confessed to the murders." Bear Man must have decided my plan was the best way to save Down.

The circle turned deadly silent, some staring at him, some at me.

"Raven only did that to protect me," Down said. "He thinks I killed them all."

In the World of the Dead

Until that moment, my only encounters with Ice Eyes had been in dreams, while I slept or was dazed after meeting Bear Man. That had allowed me to nurse a tiny element of doubt. Ice Eyes might not be real. My fate might not have been decided. My skull might not spend an eternity guarding the entrance to Willow's secret cavern. But, even while Down's proclamation still rang in my ears, I heard Ice Eyes' voice in my head. And I saw in Willow's eyes that she knew what was happening to me.

Bone

I blinked, and Down, Willow, Bear Man, and all the people of my band were gone. I was back in Ice Eyes' hut. He held me in his hands and shook me and demanded that I answer him.

"Where are you? Come back. I need you now," he said.

"What…?" I felt confused, lost. How could he summon me across all those years? Had I simply vanished from my place inside the circle only to become the skull in this strange man's hands?

He heard my baffled response. He stopped shaking and stared through those peculiar goggles into my empty eye sockets.

"She continued digging," he said. Actually, he used her name. The sounds were too peculiar to mean anything to me, but I knew who he meant—Second Woman. The one who'd become so upset about his rutting with Perfect Woman.

"She discovered a cavern behind where I found you. Another shrine. And then…" this time the name he used referred to Perfect Woman…"discovered what's back there and now both of them are in the cave, fighting. Someone will get hurt. Or the newly found artifacts might be damaged. I need your help to stop them."

I'd have laughed if I weren't so concerned about getting back to my own time, my own body, and saving the woman I loved from the situation she'd just put herself in. Just…fifteen thousand years ago.

"How do you expect me to do that?" I asked. "I have no arms, no legs, nothing but this skull. Do you expect me to think peaceful thoughts at them?"

"I don't know," he admitted. "But the other skull told me to come for you. It told me to hurry. That lives depend on it."

"The other skull? There's another skull? And it spoke to you, too?"

"We've got to hurry." He pushed his way through the hut's exits. "She said only you could help."

"She?" For a terrible moment I feared it must be Down. That the two of us had been found guilty of the murders and punished, our skulls placed near each other in The Mother's cave. Then I remembered. Willow told me The Mother had also seen a world with a strange new landscape. That she, too, had visited this place without animals.

"Yes," I said. "She's right. Take me to them now."

He did.

◇◇◇

We found the cave empty. Silence filled the cavern behind it. And darkness, though Ice Eyes dug a torch out of his clothing. One that didn't burn. No flame. Only a cold, brilliant light. It illuminated the chamber wherever Ice Eyes aimed it. It lit the rock I remembered. I could see the narrow crack. And, if I listened with my mind, I could hear the hiss of the mountain's breath.

I didn't need the torch's help, though. In fact, the dark no longer limited my vision at all. So I already knew what Ice Eyes meant when he whispered, "Oh God!"

His torch focused on a pair of booted feet extending from behind the far side of the rock. Ice Eyes set me atop the great stone and dropped to his hands and knees. Second Woman lay on the cavern's floor. He'd left me in a position where I couldn't have seen her with my eyes because the rock was in my way. But I saw well enough with my mind. Ice Eyes called her name. He bent and turned her face up toward his. She had ceased to breathe and I could tell her heart no longer beat. Her face was scratched, but only because it had struck the chamber's floor when she fell. There were no other marks on her.

"She..." he used Perfect Woman's name "...did this," Ice Eyes said. "And then she must have taken the second skull and the other pendant."

"We need that second skull," I told him. "The woman who inhabited it, she and I once knew great magics. She claimed to be a Goddess. If we can bring her back here, the two of us might be able to restore this woman to life."

I wasn't at all sure that was true. But Willow thought The Mother had revived her. Maybe The Mother could duplicate that feat here.

"You can't raise the dead," Ice Eyes gasped.

He wheezed the words, short of breath. He was over-whelmed by the loss of his woman, even if he'd considered leaving this one for the other.

"What are your choices?" I said. "I can't do it alone, but maybe with the other skull's help."

Ice Eyes was my only means of moving from place to place and I needed to find The Mother's skull. If she occupied it, maybe we could help this man. And then she might send me home to complete the task she'd set for me there. Or explain why my destiny lay here and my skull must stay forever in this terrible future.

"I know where Perfect Woman went," I said. "She has the skull with her. They're outside the cave. They've gone to that place you carried me before. Up the path to the cliff that overlooks your constructions and the snakes carrying your people's precious fuel."

Ice Eyes picked me up and we stumbled along the passage that led to the spot my skull had guarded for dark and empty ages. We passed through the cave I knew so very long ago. As we went, he regained his strength.

"There," I pointed with my mind as we emerged into daylight. He turned onto the path that circled up around the mountain and followed it.

◇◇◇

They were where I knew they'd be, on the ledge above the place where the tundra once stretched far beyond distant horizons. Perfect Woman held a skull under that filthy yellow sky, looking across the gigantic huts and the lifeless landscape.

Perfect Woman wore soft blue leggings that hugged her form, and a gray jerkin that didn't. From the way she waved her free hand at the panorama below, it was clear she could communicate with the skull she held in her other hand. The same way I communicated with Ice Eyes. I couldn't speak to Perfect Woman, but this second skull could evidently talk to both of them. And to me. Willow's voice rang in my head. No. Not Willow's, The Mother's, icy and deep, but uncharacteristically frantic.

"Raven. You've seen this horror. You must stop it. Prevent it. This cannot be allowed to happen to our world."

I would have answered but Ice Eyes lowered his shoulder and charged Perfect Woman. He might have bulled her over the wall at the edge of the cliff if he hadn't roared out in anger as we approached. "You killed her," he howled.

I already knew Perfect Woman was lithe and flexible. Well muscled, too. I'd watched those muscles ripple as she manipulated Ice Eyes into a variety of mating positions.

This time, she dodged him, and kept him from carrying me over the edge to a fall that would have smashed both of us to pieces. She did it by spinning and whipping a leg across his ankles, sweeping his feet from under him. I landed on top of him before rolling to the edge of the wall. He scrambled back to his feet. She turned and put The Mother's skull on the ground. Then the woman faced him and set her body in a way that made it clear she intended to hurt him if he came at her again. Ice Eyes wanted to do just that. I sensed the loss and anger in him, but I sensed, too, that he was no fighter. That he knew he was stronger than she but didn't have the skill to overcome her without a great deal of luck.

When he paused, Perfect Woman spoke. "I didn't kill anyone. Ask this skull." She gestured at The Mother. "Your woman was fine when we left her. We argued, sure, but that's all. Then the skull begged me to show her the world outside her cavern. That's what I was doing."

The Mother's voice agreed. "This woman didn't harm the other. We left her there, examining the chamber she just discovered. That woman wouldn't bring me outside. She wanted to record exactly how I'd been left, measure precisely where I lay among the artifacts that surrounded me. I sensed something terribly wrong out here, so I persuaded this one to let me see for myself."

"Then why is she dead?" Ice Eyes demanded.

Perfect Woman relaxed enough to shrug. "I don't know. Maybe the skull can tell you."

The Mother claimed not to know either. "But," she added, "Raven and I might be able to bring her back to life."

"Who's Raven?" Perfect Woman asked.

"I am," I said.

"Only the man can hear him," The Mother told her. "Raven is the other skull. The one this man brought here with him. Raven was a great Spirit Man in our time. With my help, he may be able to bring the other woman back from the spirit world."

I started to explain my doubts but The Mother stopped me. "Think your words only to me. The abomination they've made of my world must be undone. Only you can accomplish that."

"Me? You're The Mother, The Goddess. You do it. I'm only a fair healer and no magic maker. You know me. I'm a fake. A fraud. I know the laws. The ceremonies. But the spirits don't commune with me."

"You underestimate yourself, Raven. You will survive, your place in the band assured even after Stone inherits leadership from his father."

That confused me. "What do you mean will? Stone's been our headman for years. Or was until today. You commanded me to solve murders, including his. Will I be able to go back and do that? Be allowed to live the rest of my natural life with Down?"

"Ah," she said. "We've come to this place from different times within our own lives. Tell me the last significant event you remember."

That mystified me even more, but existing as a skull in some alien future left me inclined to accept the illogical and obey her. I told her about Stone again, about the gathering of the men just after his funeral. About how she, The Mother, had taken a place among us. How Down had told everyone I believed she was the murderer.

"I see why you're confused," she said. "I came here from a much earlier time. In my life, Willow just drowned. I brought her spirit back to her body only weeks ago. She and I are still learning to share it. Your precious Down hasn't been born yet. But, since I'm The Mother, I know much of the future. I knew you and I would meet again and that it was important for us to do so. But I knew nothing of this...this world of the dead."

"I thought you knew everything."

"Not until these people awakened me here when they broke into the inner cave. I do know, or did, that you'd out-live Stone. I know much more, as well, but this isn't the time for us to discuss our narrow lives. You've seen what they've done to our world. The vanished tundra. The absent herds. The poisonous cloud that hangs in the air. We must change all this if we're to have the future I thought I knew."

I shook my head, or tried. "How?"

"Agree with what I told them. Persuade him to take us back inside the hidden chamber. Explain that we must be near the other woman to reunite her spirit with her body. Tell him we need to go there immediately."

I didn't understand at all. Not any of it. Not how we could be here as skulls. Not how I'd come from a different time than The Mother. Not how we could do anything here that might affect what happened to us so long ago. But I agreed this place where we'd once lived had turned into a nightmare. I'd do what The Mother asked for the possibility of waking from this horror and a chance to be with Down again. I told Ice Eyes what The Mother wanted and he told Perfect Woman.

"I'll let you have all the artifacts," Ice Eyes begged Perfect Woman. "Use them for your personal profit or to enhance your position. Sell them, hide them, give them away. You can have the skulls, too. Anything, only please help me save her."

Perfect Woman agreed. They picked us up and ran, cradling us in their arms, back to the cavern where the mountain breathed.

◇◇◇

Second Woman lay where we'd left her.

"What now?" Ice Eyes asked.

"Place our skulls on the rock just above her," The Mother said. "We should each face her. And the artifacts you found in here, all of them, must be put on the rock beside us."

Ice Eyes and Perfect Woman bent and gathered colorful rocks, carved ivory, and fine tools of flint and bone. They arranged them carefully around us.

"Will this do?" Ice Eyes asked. "We've put them in the same pattern we think they formed."

"Something's missing," The Mother told me.

I extended my vision beyond what my eyes could see. I looked beyond the glare of the torches Ice Eyes and his lover used, and saw it right away. The object glowed in my mind. A pendant. The one I'd carved of Willow in the days before she became The Mother. It was in a pouch in the perfect woman's jerkin. I told Ice Eyes.

"The pendant you're hiding," he said to the girl. "Put that up here, too."

Perfect Woman flushed, but she reached into her vest, pulled it out, and placed it beside The Mother's skull.

As she gently placed the figure on the rock, I realized I'd been wrong. This was a different pendant. Very similar to the one I'd expected. But the workmanship was better. The figure, trimmer. It showed no indication of pregnancy at all, carved with small breasts and lean hips. It was Down. Exactly the way I remembered her only moments ago, an eternity away.

"Yes," The Mother said. "This one is Down. She'll be a beautiful girl, full of life and great wisdoms. The People will profit greatly from her time with them. Your carving captures her, just as the spirits tell me she'll be. Her figurine does that even better than mine."

That was when I realized the original pendant also lay in Perfect Woman's vest. Glowing, too, though not nearly as bright. I told Ice Eyes.

"Both figurines," he said.

The girl didn't argue. She put it beside Down's on the rock that breathed.

"How can there be two?" I asked The Mother. "I haven't carved an image of Down."

"Perhaps you have yet to carve it," she replied. "But whether you'll get that opportunity will be determined by what happens now."

"You mean whether we can bring the woman back to life?"

"Not exactly," The Mother said. "Watch."

As she said it, Perfect Woman lost her balance. She knocked a few of the colored stones off the rock as she tried to catch herself, then crumpled to her knees on the cavern's floor.

"Something's wrong," she said. "I feel dizzy."

"Me, too." Ice Eyes sat heavily beside her. "What's happening to us?"

"Can you get up?" The Mother asked.

The girl made a half-hearted effort, then sprawled on the floor.

Ice Eyes struggled mightily. "What have you done?" He crawled in our direction. "Stop it. Stop it now or I'll smash you both."

"We haven't done anything," The Mother said. "You brought yourselves to a sacred place we were unable to guard from you. You looted it. Had you heeded the warnings we represented, you would never have entered this place."

That was true. They brought themselves here to begin with. But they'd returned at our bidding. Because we promised to try to save the dead woman.

The Mother spoke again. "This chamber is filled with the breath of Grandmother Earth. The same breath that you steal to give yourselves every convenience. In the process, you've destroyed the partners with whom you were meant to share the Earth. Because of your greed, it's only appropriate that Grandmother Earth's breath poisons you. You have to leave here if you want to live. But it's too late. Now you'll both die."

Perfect Woman managed a whisper. "Help me," she begged Ice Eyes.

Ice Eyes looked into my eye sockets. "I meant you no harm."

He was right. He'd expected to benefit from me, and he'd been willing to trade our artifacts and skulls for Perfect Woman's help. But he'd only wanted to save a life. And earlier, to know who we were so he could tell our story. I tried to think him to his feet. I'd been able to hurl a spear point at Perfect Woman once. Not very effectively. Maybe I could help him move. And I did, a little, though he fought me because he wanted to take Perfect Woman to safety with him. It was too late for her. Not that I cared about helping her, anyway. Her body, however perfect, had been a vessel harboring only greed and self-interest.

Perfect Woman stopped struggling. Her breath came shallow and fast. She wouldn't last long. I shoved him the other way. He collapsed after a pace or two. I scooted him a little farther before I realized I couldn't possibly get him out in time.

Perfect Woman shuddered as she breathed her last.

"If I can still get them out of here," I asked The Mother, "away from Grandmother Earth's breath, can you give them life again? Can we?"

"No, Raven. It's rare that I can restore any spirit to the body it just left. These people have only bodies and minds. No spirits. They're empty shells. I can't do anything for these three. Nor can you, even though you have more powers than I."

"No, I don't," I protested.

"Your mind can grasp hold of things here. Move them. The way you just moved the man, though it was too late for him. I can't do that."

I was shocked. "Me? I have powers you don't? How can that be? There aren't any spirits here to help me. Only you, and you're The Goddess. I'm just a man."

"Not just a man, Raven. How do you think you came to be here, outside your body, outside your time? Existing only inside your skull? What normal man can do that?"

"I don't understand."

"You were chosen, Raven. By all the spirits. We aided you, guided you, even let you deny us. How do you think you reached that moment you just left in your camp? Leading your band? Seeking to discover who killed men that preferred to see you dead?"

I didn't believe her, and yet...

"I know," she said. "You still aren't sure who the murderer is. And you can't understand about the boy with red hair and why I call that a murder, too. Think about it, Raven. He wasn't suitable for Down. Only you could help her become the next vessel for my spirit. When Willow dies, Down will share her body with me. She, too, will become Earth Mother."

"I lost one woman to you. Why would I let you take another?"

"Because I'll let you keep this one to yourself. I'll only share her eyes. I won't rule her mind and body. It's clear to me, if we're to avoid this future, I must have Down's help. And yours. We have to learn and understand the flaw that lies within ourselves. The one that led here. Together, we may help guide the spirits to regain control and preserve our world for as long as possible."

"Why not preserve it forever?"

I felt her shake her head, though neither of us moved. "Nothing is forever, Raven. Not our Earth, and not this place. Now is the time for you to end it."

I actually turned my skull so our eye sockets stared into each other's. "How?"

"In our time, I showed you this place, right? I showed you a flame burning on the stone, put it out and relit it, so you understood how Grandmother Earth's breath burns.

"Yes. That happened."

"Study the image of Down you may create. Remember the profusion of life that migrated past this place. Consider what's outside this cavern now. Then move a piece of flint with your mind. Scratch it on the rock. The spirit of fire has been waiting here for as long as you and I. Waiting to end this world. To turn this mountain into a tower of flame and destroy what Ice Eyes' people built beside it to steal Grandmother Earth's breath. The flame will free the breath they've captured and ignite it, too. Without this terrible place, and without the plants and animals they've killed, they can't survive."

"I don't want to kill people. Not even people who'd do this to their world."

"You won't kill anyone. These are only empty bodies. They have no sprits. They aren't People. They're soulless, like mosquitoes, sucking Grandmother Earth dry. You can't hurt them or the world they created because they already destroyed everything that's important. All that's left is evil. It must burn."

"Then what happens to us?" I asked.

"I don't know," she confessed. "Perhaps we die with this world. Wouldn't that be preferable to remaining in it while its occupants finish committing the suicide of the flesh already done to their spirits? Think about that second pendant. You haven't carved it yet. Maybe…"

I looked at Down's image. I remembered the lifeless world outside. I agreed. It needed to end. But I didn't think I could do it.

"You must," The Mother screamed.

"I can't." I answered. "You won't tolerate murder in our band, but you'd have me murder every inhabitant of an entire world?"

"I told you," she howled. "There are no longer people here to murder. Just meat, empty sacks of walking flesh."

Ice Eyes managed to pull himself back to the edge of the rock. He reached, at first, I thought, for me. He grabbed a piece of flint instead.

"She's right," he said. "We should've saved the animals, shared our world with them. You showed me your world. It had a balance ours lost. There's nothing left worth saving."

He swung the flint toward the fracture in the stone.

"See," I told The Mother. "You're wrong. This one has a soul."

The flint met the stone and sparked. The world turned brighter than the sun. I felt myself fracture into splinters, then a haze of dust, slipping beyond thought, but still feeling wonder as the fire's spirit joined Grandmother Earth's breath and consumed everything.

Confrontation

Willow watched me. No, not Willow. Those cold hard eyes belonged to The Mother. We were back in the band's council circle, but I could tell she knew where I'd been and what happened there.

World-consuming flame had been replaced by a small, dung-fueled fire. My band sat around it, intent on saving their world instead of destroying it. And Down's statement, that I believed she'd committed the murders, still echoed in everyone's ears. My eyes were on The Mother, but I saw Down just over her shoulder.

"You killed them."

I didn't realize I'd said it out loud until I saw Down look away. She must have thought I meant Tall Pine and Hair on Fire and Stone since I'd said it here, in this circle. She couldn't know it was The Mother I accused, or that victims existed in some distant future. And yet, I knew it wasn't The Mother who killed them or even Ice Eyes when he scraped the flint. I had done it. I'd convinced Ice Eyes of his people's terrible crime. Because he sympathized with me, believed in an idealized nobility of The People and our way of life, he annihilated his own world to try to preserve ours.

"Oh, Raven," Down said, "if you don't believe me anymore, I can't think of any reason not to confess. It doesn't matter, now, whether I live or die."

"No," The Mother said. "That's not what Raven means. I'm the one he accuses, but the crime he speaks of took place in another world. The spirits let the two of us travel there to see it. Its people were a terrible, evil race, a great threat to us all. I did kill them, with Raven's help. We made that sacrifice for the good of Grandmother Earth and all her People and animals."

The band sat stunned in rapt silence. They didn't understand a thing, of course, but they trusted that what she said was important to them. And it was. After a fashion, it was even true.

"But now, Raven, it's time to return to the murders in this band. You still have another duty to perform for The People—to reveal the identity of the murderer."

I nodded. I paused to face Down again and give her a reassuring smile. And I noticed poor Blue Flower standing at her side. She must be feeling especially lost if she had sought solace beside Stone's daughter. That she was there, surprised me. But not nearly as much as the willow branch doll, clasping a flower, that she held to her breast.

I took a deep breath. I'd been so naive, though no one had ever trained me for this. "All right." I finally knew who, and why. And how to reveal and prove it, all at the same time.

I reached into the pouch I wore around my neck and pulled out Tall Pine's bone. If it had power, I needed it now.

I'd seen how easily The Mother manipulated Ice Eyes and Perfect Woman, persuading them to go back into a chamber filled with a poison that would kill them. I thought about my visits to Ice Eyes, and how The Mother influenced Ice Eyes through me until he willingly destroyed his own society. In my frame of reference, I'd just witnessed her kill Perfect Woman. Maybe Second Woman, too. And, through Ice Eyes and myself, perhaps everyone in the huts below the cavern and the places reached by those snakes carrying the Earth's breath. Possibly, an entire world. If she could do that, I knew she was capable of almost anything. I remembered what she'd told me about Hair on Fire. *"He wasn't suitable for Down. Only you could help her become the next vessel for my spirit."*

"I know the murderer's identity," I said. I stepped around the fire and looked straight into The Mother's face. I tossed her Tall Pine's bone. "You. You killed them all."

The entire band gasped—a single shared breath—but one immediately torn apart by a deafening roar.

"Raven lies," Bear Man shouted. "He's the killer. He told me so himself. Do you deny that, Raven?"

I shook my head. "But what about the moccasin prints we found beside our headman's body? Look at Blue Flower. She came to this council barefooted."

Bear Man didn't answer, but Willow said, "Go on."

I pointed at Blue Flower. "Where did you get that doll?"

She shook her head, torn briefly from her grief by my unexpected question.

"Under his body," she said. "I tried to lift him up and make him be all right. But he was dead. I thought he made this doll to show me he loved me. You see, it has a blue flower."

"Yes. Would you please bring it to me?"

She did, though she seemed reluctant to let me have it. The doll was virtually identical to the one Gentle Breeze had found on Tall Pine's body. And it was tied using the same unusual knot on that one, with its yellow flower, as on the one with the bloody head that had been hidden in my bedding.

"Does this look familiar?" I asked Gentle Breeze.

"It looks just like the one I found on Tall Pine," she said, "but surely you're not accusing Blue Flower of being the killer... and our witch."

I turned to Bear Man. He shook with rage and I wondered whether he'd pick up his club and bash my head in the moment I got close to him. But there was one more item I needed. I stepped in front of him, bent, and pulled Blue Flower's moccasins from his belt. I walked over to stand in front of Bull Hump and Takes Risks, the only fighters who might be strong enough to keep me alive.

"Look at these knots." I showed them the knots tying the doll and the moccasins before them. "Have you ever seen someone tie knots like this before?"

They hadn't.

I tossed them to The Mother. "How about you?"

The great bear came charging from his place in the circle, batting men aside. People flew everywhere, some from the force of his passage, others trying to get out of his way. But this bear didn't lumber on four legs. He ran upright, on two. And straight toward me, swinging his massive club. No great bear at all, just Bear Man, but every bit as deadly as his name and nearly twice my size.

I stepped behind the fire to make him change direction. The Mother had told me all the spirits were with me. That I was a great magician, capable of feats even she couldn't perform. I wished I believed her.

Instead, I remembered how Perfect Woman, smaller and weaker than Ice Eyes, dodged his charge and swept his feet out from under him with a spinning kick. I had nothing to lose. I tried it. Imagine my surprise when it worked.

Bear Man landed on hands and knees directly in front of The Mother.

"Enough," she told him. "You aren't the instrument of my will. You may think you kill for me, but you kill in spite of me. It must stop here."

Her words stripped away some of his rage and made him moan in agony. But only for a moment.

"I am The Mother's son." he shouted. "I shall be her inheritor. I'll take what I want and anyone who stands in my way cannot be allowed to live."

He scooped a hand into the fire and threw flaming coals at Bull Hump and Takes Risks. They dodged away. Bear Man leaped to his feet and came for me again and I knew my kick wouldn't work a second time. He raised the club. For a foolish moment I felt pleased. At least he'd smash my skull, preventing the fate I so dreaded. Just as he got to me, he fell dead at my feet.

Down danced out from under him as he collapsed, leaving the spear she'd borrowed from Takes Risks embedded in Bear Man's flesh. She'd gone in low and thrust up from beneath his rib cage and into his heart, the way she'd seen me kill the mammoth.

I shook my head in disbelief as Down came into my arms. "Now," she whispered, "there's finally one I can honestly admit to having killed."

"As you should." The Mother stood, her voice tinged with sadness. "One murderer has been punished. An accomplice has been revealed, as she needed to be. But I'm that accomplice. I foresaw Bear Man's crimes and, because of the dangers we all faced, did nothing to prevent them. Because I'm The Mother, however, the punishments that apply to you don't apply to me."

"Why not?" I said. "Tall Pine was a threat to Down's well-being but you have need of Down. So Bear Man stole her garrote and eliminated Tall Pine. He shot Bull Hump. You sent him to shoot the mammoth to attract the animal's attention so Hair on Fire would die. Bear Man succeeded, but he only nicked the mammoth and turned her attention before the arrow accidentally ricocheted into Bull Hump. Bear Man wanted Down. He persuaded Stone to get rid of me, but you needed me today, so you let Bear Man finish Stone."

"True." The Mother shrugged. "But Bear Man never acted on my orders. As for Down, I told him he couldn't have her. It would be incest. Bear Claw was my father, and Stone's. When you revealed him, Bear Man decided to take control of the band by force. He was a fool to think I'd allow that. In the end, I let Down punish him."

"He killed," I said, "and though you can say it was for Down and for power, you didn't stop him because he accomplished what you wanted. You're as guilty as Bear Man."

I didn't give her time to answer. I ripped the spear out of Bear Man's body and hurled it into The Mother's.

It didn't quite get there. Snow flew out of nowhere and plucked the spear out of the air, stopping it no more than a hand's breadth from The Mother's flesh. My faithful dog carried it out of the circle, madly wagging his tail, delighted by this new sport he'd found to play with me.

"Yes, I'm as guilty," The Mother answered. "But I'm not subject to punishment by you. If I've done wrong, my fellow spirits will discipline me."

She stood, raised her arms, and addressed everyone. "The wound that threatened our band, and all The People, is healed. Let the murderer lie where he revealed himself. Let the animals and carrion birds feed on his flesh and spread his bones so it will soon be as if he never existed. Let our band move to my mountain immediately and reunite. Once there, we will rejoice. Thanks to Raven and Down, The People are healed."

The Mother's Wisdom

It took another day to move ourselves and our goods to The Mother's mountain. I had mixed feelings about going back. At least I no longer expected to die there, or not soon. If she'd wanted my life, I finally understood, The Mother could have let Bear Man take it anytime. If she still wanted my skull, she wouldn't need it soon.

One reason we went back to the mountain was because The Mother's camp was better provisioned even than ours. The Mother, who seemed to have become Willow again, told us they had more than enough food for a huge celebration. Every band that passed left the choicest pieces of their latest kills when they learned The Mother resided there. The river below the cave yielded delicious fish and its banks were bordered with edible plants, roots, and berries.

On the day after our newly recombined band celebrated the murderer's discovery and Down's act to cleanse us of him, Willow appeared at our tent. There was no hint of The Mother's hardness in her eyes or voice. She reached out and gently took both of us by the hands. "Come, walk with me."

She led us upstream, along the gravel bars at the water's edge.

"I know you still believe The Mother was guilty of killing our band members," she said.

I agreed. "You told me, or she did, how the spirits protected me. How they saved Down for me, and then you. Everything we accomplished seems to have been a result of Bear Man's violent acts. Acts which resulted in what you wanted. I can't see the will of the spirits in what happened."

"The will of the spirits is hard for men to understand. We are rid of evil, self-absorbed men. A murderer was punished. An unacceptable future was averted. Only temporarily, The Mother tells me, but these were great accomplishments and they required a great cost."

"And yet you could have stopped your son anytime."

"The Mother's son or mine? And, no, she didn't stop him, nor did I. Even a Goddess finds it difficult to kill her own child."

I moved to my next question. "How could you be certain Down would kill Bear Man and save me?"

Willow laughed. "The Mother isn't as infallible as she pretends. She thought Bear Man would kill you."

I was taken aback. "Then how would Down give me that son you promised?"

"Because she's already pregnant, of course," Willow said. "Why do you think she stopped bleeding?"

Down threw her arms around me. "You don't think I'd let the father of my child be snatched away from me so easily, do you?"

My head swam, but I managed to hug Down, and the son she carried, with as much fervor as she hugged me.

◇◇◇

Willow led us to a place where the river had created a beach of small rocks and sand on its rush to the sea.

"Pick up a stone, Raven," Willow said. "Toss it far out into the water near the stream's center."

I did so. "And what great truth have I just helped you demonstrate?"

Willow smiled and lightly punched my shoulder the way she would have decades before.

"The Mother asked me to point out the ripples your rock caused. They spread forward in every direction from where it struck. The current stops them from going back. Think of the current as time, moving from the present into the future. Except time's flow would extend beyond these banks forever. Your ripples could make an infinite journey in any direction except backwards. The Mother says it's the same with what we do in our lives. Every choice leads to all manner of possible outcomes and affects things we never dream of. There are many possible futures. Some are disasters, like the one we saw. She and the spirits needed the help of a special man to stop it, someone who always tries to do what's right, even when it isn't convenient."

Flattery, I thought, exaggerating what I'd done.

Down took my arm. "They made a good choice," she said, making everything seem worthwhile.

"The Mother believed Bear Man would take matters into his own hands," Willow said, "but the decisions he made were his own. The future she expected didn't have to happen. And some of it didn't."

Down turned to face Willow. "What was Bear Man after? Why did he want me?"

Willow's face grew sad again. "Bear Man thought he was superior to The People. He enjoyed exercising the power of life and death. He planned to take you so The Mother couldn't have you. He resented The Mother and was foolish enough to think he could replace her and assume her power."

"Who will The Mother pick for our headman now?" Down asked.

"Raven, of course. But she won't pick him. The band will do that."

I objected. "Wait. Are you talking about me? The band won't accept me as headman."

"You're wrong," Willow said. "You've already led them. The band meets tonight and they'll choose you. Who else would they pick? You saved them from Bear Man. You even challenged The Mother. None of them are brave enough for that."

"Well, say you're right. What happens then? Do we spend the rest of our winters in this place, guarding Grandmother Earth's breath from a repeat of that dangerous future?"

Willow shrugged. "I suppose that's our destiny."

"No it's not." Down picked up a rock and hurled it in the stream. Before its ripples moved far, she threw a handful of sand after it. The original ripples broke, scattered, and found new courses.

"It's not just mighty acts or great spirits that affect the future's ripples," Down said. "As soon as you're named headman, Raven, you'll march us on the trail the animals took, south through the mountains. Before the seasons change, we can be far from this accursed place. Soon, no one will ever dream of bringing skulls back. If your skulls aren't buried here, those strangers from the future can't find them and you won't have to destroy their world."

Willow laughed. "See why you and The Mother need this woman, Raven? She's right. She may not prevent that future, or one like it, but each of our acts alters what will be, in small or large ways. If we follow the animals, we'll certainly alter the course of our own ripples. Who knows what may eventually happen?"

◇◇◇

We took the pass through the mountains on the heels of the animals. Spent our first winter in a wide valley bordered by glaciers. The mountains blocked the worst of the storms and many animals wintered in the valley with us. We took only the ones we needed and thanked each animal's spirit for their gift to us. We survived that winter far better than we deserved after such a long delay.

My first child, a son of course, was born on the trail south from that valley. He had such pale eyes. And something I thought I recognized behind them. I asked Down if we could call him Ice Eyes. She agreed, and Willow didn't object.

By then, Down wore an image of herself, better carved and more of a likeness than the one I'd made for Willow. And Willow wore her own image again. My second carving depicted Down as lean and young and extraordinarily beautiful, and, though it wasn't the way I'd seen the figurine in the cavern of The Mother's Breath, I carved it thick with child, the way Down decided she wanted to be depicted.

I'm a very old man now. My hands are gnarled and twisted and painful, incapable of more carvings. Someone else would have to fashion the one I saw in the cave so long ago…so far in the future.

Our band follows the herds across lush rolling grasslands where rivers lined with trees twist among golden hills, rich with nuts and roots, fruit and berries. We hunt the nearby mountains, too, thick with fragrant pine forests and clear cool streams. We've found The Mother's bounty everywhere. Our band has grown and prospered. As it should, since Willow carried The Mother's spirit and Down became a skilled Spirit Woman.

Before she died, Willow asked to speak to me.

I sat in front of a tent, no longer able to hunt for myself, but fattened by doting children. "Does The Mother require more of us?"

"No." Willow eased her shrunken frame to sit on the soft grass beside me, warming herself at our fire. "The Mother hasn't spoken to me in years."

"Did you offend her?"

Willow shook her head. "She believes both of us endured enough."

"You mean when we were skulls."

"Were we, really? I've come to hope that was a terrible nightmare you and I shared. Not reality."

Wouldn't that be wonderful? Wonderful, too, if there were no Mother to link spirits with Down.

"But just in case," Willow said, "I'd like to ask a favor."

"Of course."

"When I die, don't bury me. Burn me. Burn me until my bones are fragile enough to crumble into ash. Then spread me on the wind, so those people, or their counterparts, can never find me."

We did as she asked. And even though I'm no longer so afraid of that future Ice Eyes, Down has promised me the same favor.

Down didn't inherit The Mother's spirit after Willow died. I was relieved. I'd had enough of The Mother. But because of her, we'd prospered, enjoying an amazing string of successful years. Leading a band that had the reputation of enjoying The Mother's favor proved almost effortless, especially when she no longer made demands on us. After Willow's death, representatives of other bands still came seeking The Mother's blessing. Down gave them private audiences, instead. She always wore that oh-so-pregnant image of herself—one more ripple away from my dreams of being a skull.

I never dreamed such dreams again. Nor anything like them. And neither did Willow or Down...or so they always claimed.

Now, as I lie dying, I dream of sharing my story with those who need to hear it in a fashion impossible for me to describe. Warning them of the flaws to which we, The People, are susceptible. Flaws that might lead us back to another doomed future.

Down purifies me with a pinch of pollen and the brush of a grass whisk when I wake from those dreams. She tells me The Mother will let me share my warning.

But The Mother couldn't have told her that. Or could she? Perhaps it's only another dream. No matter. My time ends. Will my spirit join friends around those countless campfires in the sky? Will my soul return again and again? And one day share my story? I close my eyes and wonder if...

Afterword &
Acknowledgements

Once upon a time, I spent a summer on the North Slope of the Brooks Range in Alaska, one hundred and forty-three miles north of the Arctic Circle. The land was every bit as beautiful and harsh as I've depicted it in this novel. Within hours of disembarking from a floatplane, two of us encountered a great bear. Like Raven and Down. A grizzly, in our case. We were better clothed and armed, but we didn't shoot, or intend to shoot. Bears weren't what we hunted there, and we knew our chances of stopping a charging grizzly were next to nil. Fortunately, this one, after an uncomfortably close inspection, chose to go elsewhere.

We spent ninety days in the field, from mid-June to the end of August. It rained two days out of three and snowed about once a week. Temperatures ranged from ninety-four to nine degrees Fahrenheit. While there, we saw more bears as well as moose, caribou, wolverines, foxes, dall sheep, ground squirrels, ptarmigan, songbirds, a host of waterfowl, and grayling (a form of arctic freshwater salmon). We saw no wolves, just their tracks in the same places we frequented. Ghosts.

Those invisible wolves lead me to something else about the Arctic I've tried to portray in these pages. There exists an oddness that's hard to explain. It's a sense that magic would be normal there. That usual rules don't apply. That you could climb a ridge one morning and see a band of prehistoric big-game hunters creeping up on the mammoths feeding at the edge of the lake below. Or watch a herd of caribou thick enough to blanket the Earth in their tens of thousands—something we actually witnessed.

Those familiar with this landscape know how commonly it affects the people, both positively and negatively, who live there or visit it. Look up Arctic Hysteria. Then apply the term to us, if you think it's appropriate.

We were forty-seven miles from a geological field camp at Umiat on the Colville River, and forty-four miles from the nearest permanently occupied human habitation, an Eskimo village at Anaktuvuk Pass. Yet we heard voices. On several still evenings, while curtains of fog draped the tundra, we clearly heard conversations. We could never make out the words. Maybe geologists or hunters were somewhere in our area. If so, the occasional floatplanes that brought us supplies and visitors didn't know about them. Maybe conditions were right and allowed the sound of voices to carry extraordinary distances. Or maybe Raven's band passed nearby.

One member of our party looked up and saw a woman in skins and furs standing beside the creek where we did most of our work. Could it have been Down, perhaps? Or The Mother, gracing him with her presence—or warning us away—before she disappeared into thin air?

I loved my brief time above the Arctic Circle. That summer was among the most valuable learning experiences of my life. I wish I'd gone back. The memory of that place still haunts me. Sometimes, I think if I could return to that ridge I mentioned earlier, I could cross it, go down, and join that band of mammoth hunters. I know exactly where The Mother's cave is now, though we couldn't find it while we were there. Maybe, all these years later, I've begun to understand the words I heard whispering through the fog and shared them here with you.

For those who want to know how accurately The People's culture has been portrayed in this novel, there's no way to know for certain. These undocumented immigrants to the New World probably carried a Clovis-like toolkit. But permafrost archaeology doesn't cooperate with confirming that. Frozen soil churns, tumbling artifacts, and other materials deposited on the surface, moving them inconveniently up, down, and sideways. We, for instance, found the remains of a mammoth tusk that had clearly been cut by humans. Who knows when, since Eskimos harvested mammoth ivory for tools and artwork long after the last of the mammoths died. But we found a mammoth tooth there as well. That would seem to indicate the rest of the beast lay nearby. We began excavating in search of it and found nothing. Nothing except frozen soil, and when we'd return, a trench filled with permafrost melt that had to be bailed out before another inch or so of muck could be scraped from the bottom. One or two more bailing sessions might have uncovered it. Or a thousand more might not. I was always certain it lay close by. If we'd only known exactly where or how deep to dig, we'd have found it along with the weapons the big-game hunters used to bring it down.

What we did find was a collection of unusual artifacts, far more primitive than Clovis, in the gravels of one small creek. Those tools were absent from adjacent waterways. They're a fascinating hint of what might have been the tools of some of the first people to enter the Americas. Or not.

I considered and rejected using more formal language in the novel to indicate that The People spoke in a different and simpler way. In the end, I decided they'd have had a large and complex vocabulary, and when they spoke to each other, the patterns they heard would have been as full of contractions and shortcuts as modern English. I'll have to admit the bear/bare pun probably wouldn't have worked the way I used it. Something quite similar might have, however. And tribal peoples are noted for their earthy sense of humor.

I suspect I've been too generous with many tools my version of The People had available. Atalatls, sure. Bows and arrows, maybe. Wine, not likely, especially for immigrants traversing such a difficult environment. The same goes for the penicillin-like mold. We do know, however, that prehistoric societies studied and understood their habitats thoroughly. Items with healing properties, and alcohol—for its purely medicinal properties, of course—were independently discovered early and often. And those fermented beverages never lost their popularity.

There are no Paleolithic ivory Venus figurines in the New World. But The Mother, The Goddess of the animals, was certainly here. Maybe Raven independently invented an art form common to another place and time. Or maybe we haven't found the ivory Venus carvings of the Americas yet.

Thanks to my readers and editors—Annette Rogers, Barbara Peters, Elizabeth Gunn, Susan Cummins Miller, Barbara Hayes, J. Carson Black, and Janet Dailey. Life has been so complicated during the writing of this novel, that I might never have gotten this mess sorted out without their kind assistance. For any errors that remain, the author alone is responsible.

JMH

Sedna Creek, AK, and Tucson, AZ

To receive a free catalog of Poisoned Pen Press titles, please contact us in one of the following ways:

Phone: 1-800-421-3976
Facsimile: 1-480-949-1707
Email: info@poisonedpenpress.com
Website: www.poisonedpenpress.com

Poisoned Pen Press
6962 E. First Ave. Ste 103
Scottsdale, AZ 85251